ACCLAIM FOR THE HOME CRAFTING MYSTERY SERIES

Something Borrowed, Something Bleu

"This series continues to add depth to its engaging cast of characters, and the home-crafting details remain a delight and an inspiration."—*Booklist*

"Witty, suspenseful, and very engaging, *Something Borrowed, Something Bleu* is a winner." —*The Coloradoan*

"Likable characters and an easy-to-follow plot that doesn't require knowledge of previous entries in the series are a plus."—*Publishers Weekly*

Spin a Wicked Web

"Cozy up for a finely crafted mystery—lots of twists and tangles, a most entertaining yarn." —Laura Childs, author of *Death by Darjeeling: A Tea Shop Mystery*

"Cricket's your ticket to the lighter side of murder in her latest crafty mystery."—Mary Daheim, author of the Alpine Mystery series and the Bed and Breakfast Mystery series

"Interested fans can watch Sophie Mae's detecting expertise and her love life develop while absorbing all the information they could possibly want about the joys of spinning."—*Kirkus Reviews*

Heaven Preserve Us

"McRae writes about characters that we really care about... Sophie Mae and her friends deserve many more adventures."—*Booklist*

"Strong characters and [a] unique plot... spellbinding."—*Sydney Star Observer*

"Nicely paced without any time wasted, *Heaven Preserve Us* does a fine job of leading the readers through the investigation with no false starts or cheap side trips...solid and entertaining."—Reviewing the Evidence

Lye in Wait

~ _Lye in Wait_ was a finalist for the 2007 _ForeWord Magazine_ Book of the Year Award ~

"[A] new tweak on the cozy, complete with credibly written characters possessing enough appealing eccentricities to keep readers happy."—*Booklist*

"McRae crafts strong characters [and] spins a credible, enjoyable plot."—*Library Journal*

"A fresh new voice, wry and cheeky, speaks in Cricket McRae's *Lye in Wait*, a clever mystery with a romantic twist and an ingenious resolution."—Larry Karp, author of *First Do No Harm* and the Thomas Purdue Mystery Series

Wined and Died

"McRae's ... latest offers a tutorial on mead and a dash of soapmaking, all wrapped around a credible mystery."—*Kirkus Reviews*

"[A] delightful cozy ... fans will again appreciate the extensive knowledge McRae shares about traditional crafts and skills."—*Booklist*

"Wine, suspense sprinkled with humor and an intriguing plot will take you away anytime you want to escape."—*The Coloradoan*

Deadly Row to Hoe

OTHER BOOKS BY CRICKET MCRAE

Lye in Wait

Heaven Preserve Us

Spin a Wicked Web

Something Borrowed, Something Bleu

Wined and Died

A Home Crafting Mystery

Deadly Row to Hoe

Cricket McRae

FIRST EDITION
First Printing, 2012

Book design and format by Donna Burch
Cover design by Lisa Novak
Cover illustrator: Robin Moline/Jennifer Vaughn Artist Agent
Editing by Connie Hill

Midnight Ink, an imprint of Llewellyn Worldwide Ltd.

This is a work of fiction. Names, characters, places, and incidents are either the product of the author's imagination or are used fictitiously, and any resemblance to actual persons (living or dead), business establishments, events, or locales is entirely coincidental.

Library of Congress Cataloging-in-Publication Data

McRae, Cricket.
Deadly row to hoe : a home crafting mystery / Cricket McRae. — 1st ed.
p. cm.
ISBN 978-0-7387-3308-1
1. Reynolds, Sophie Mae (Fictitious character)—Fiction. 2. Farmers—Fiction. 3. Women—Crimes against—Fiction. 4. Washington (State)—Fiction. I. Title.
PS3613.C58755D43 2012
813'.6—dc23 2012026557

Midnight Ink
Llewellyn Worldwide Ltd.
2143 Wooddale Drive
Woodbury, MN 55125-2989
www.midnightinkbooks.com

Printed in the United States of America

This book is dedicated to small farmers and backyard gardeners everywhere.

ACKNOWLEDGMENTS

I'm so grateful to the many people who helped create this book and get it into the hands of readers. The skilled and hardworking team of Terri Bischoff, Connie HIll, Courtney Colton, Donna Burch, and Lisa Novak at Midnight Ink are great to work with and did their usual awesome job. My writing buddies Mark and Bob, bless their hearts, have read and critiqued this mystery series from the beginning, and the ladies of the Old Town Writing Group—Janet, Laura, Dana, other Laura, Carrie and Sarah—provided encouragement and kept me going when deadlines loomed. Kevin, as always, loaded on the love and support and the occasional, "Shouldn't you be writing?"

Community Supported Agriculture is going strong where I live, and I'm thankful to be able to buy the majority of our food from local farmers and ranchers. Among the many who provide the food we eat I thank the folks at Happy Heart Farm, Cresset Farm, Windsor Dairy, Quatrix Aquaponics, and Jodar Farms for chatting with me and giving farm tours. Theirs is tough yet vital work. Friends of Happy Heart Farm also raises funds to provide local low-income families with some of the best organic foods available. Nice work, guys!

ONE

Chickens gabbled and pigs rooted through the compost pile outside the dark and dusty shack. To the left, a long greenhouse soaked up the summer light, heating the tomato vines, melons, and squash. On the other side, afternoon sun shone down on sprawling pumpkins, pickling cucumbers, and thirty-five feet of berry-heavy canes. The sound of a car starting up in the parking lot signaled the departure of a farm stand customer. Voices drifted from the direction of the open field.

Squinting at the thermometer in the dim light of the shed, I tried to remember whether 98.1° was a high or low basal body temperature. Kind of high, I seemed to remember from reading the brief instructions that came with the device. But I was supposed to be keeping track so I'd know what was high or low for me. More research was definitely in order.

I rose from the pile of burlap bags I'd been sitting on in the vegetable distribution shed at Turner Farm. Tomorrow morning volunteers would be shoving green beans and peppers, eggplants and ears of just-picked corn into them for pickup by the members who had purchased a CSA membership share. Community Supported Agriculture had finally come to Cadyville, Washington, and my best friend Meghan Bly and I were right in the middle of it.

The whiff of tomato leaves rose from my fingers as I brought the thermometer closer. 98.1°, huh. Well, this whole temperature tracking thing was new, as was the idea of actually trying to get pregnant instead of simply waiting for it to happen naturally. But once my husband and I decided to go ahead and have a baby, I was anxious to get on with it. Let's face it: I wasn't getting any younger.

98.1°. Maybe I should call Barr. Just in case. Couldn't hurt, right? I smiled to myself.

A scream lacerated the air. Shoving the instrument in my pocket, I jerked the door open and bolted outside. I knew that voice, and Meghan was not prone to screaming. From the corner of my eye I saw Tom Turner loping across the field, heading toward the far end of the greenhouse.

With a knot of dread twisting through my solar plexus, I sprinted toward the plastic-covered tunnel and down the central aisle, past the indeterminate tomato vines I'd been tying up half an hour earlier. Their heirloom fruit glowed in my peripheral vision like multihued gems. Exiting at the other end, I saw Tom had veered to the right, toward Meghan and the towering pile of compost.

Wisps of steam rose from the heap of decaying matter, visible even in the seventy-degree day. An ancient John Deere track hoe sat quietly to one side, ready to fire up and give the compost a good toss. Meghan stood hugging herself. Tears cut dirty streaks through the dust on her face.

Without warning she ran toward the pile and swung her arms in a shooing gesture. As I neared, a low mewling sound came from someplace deep inside her chest. I'd never heard Meghan do that, and it frightened me. The young pig we'd named Arnold Ziffel ran off, dragging away a purple cabbage leaf half as big as he was and snorting happily.

When I reached her side, Meghan spun and stared at me with hands on her hips. Her chin quivered, and the muscles along her jaw line clenched and unclenched.

My eyes widened. "Good Lord! What happened? Are you all right?"

Without breaking eye contact, she pointed at the ground about ten feet away, where Tom Turner now stood with his arms crossed and shoulders hunched.

I tore my gaze away from hers and directed it downward. It took a moment to make out what I was looking at. Then the recognizable pattern of a waffle-soled boot emerged.

Now why would . . . ?

Following the line of the boot, I saw it was well-worn, scuffed at both heel and toe. It stopped ankle high, revealing a sock.

A dirty but festive green-and-blue-striped sock, in fact. Which appeared to have a leg in it.

My jaw slackened as realization dawned. My hand crept to my throat, and I looked back at Meghan. After a couple of tries, I finally got the words out. "Is that what I think it is?"

She clamped her bottom lip between her teeth, and her hand rose so her shaking finger pointed straight at me.

"What? I didn't put it there!"

The sock disappeared into the fifteen-foot-high mountain of vegetable scraps and manure slowly turning themselves into fine, dark dirt. The stripes made me think wildly of the Wicked Witch of the East, but those hiking boots were about as far away from ruby slippers as you could get.

Meghan's swallow was audible. "I'm not the one who's supposed to find dead people, Sophie Mae. *You* are."

"Hey!" But it rang true. Suspicious deaths had seemed to crop up around me ever since I'd discovered the neighborhood handyman dead on our basement floor. But the "supposed to" bothered me.

Elbowing past her, I knelt and touched the side of the boot. Pushed at it gently. Tried to wiggle it, just to make sure. Yep. That was a leg all right. It was stiff as all get out.

"This is some kind of joke, right?" Tom Turner said.

I peered up at his lanky, overalled form silhouetted against the August-blue sky. "If it is, I don't get it."

His eyes met mine, and I watched as the knowledge deepened. There really was a body buried in his compost. He glanced at the John Deere, then seemed to think better of it. He jogged off again, this time toward the tool shed.

"Oh, my God. Do you think she could be alive?" Sudden panic infused Meghan's voice.

Shaking my head, I stood. "I don't see how." I didn't mention how the leg had felt when I'd tried to move it.

But new tears had replaced my friend's glare, and she began pawing in the compost, pushing it aside by the armful as I took out my cell phone and dialed 911. I told the male operator who answered to send an ambulance along with law enforcement, just in case, and to hurry.

"Sure thing, Sophie Mae. I bet Barr's not gonna like this."

I ignored the disturbing note of glee in his voice. "Just send your people out, okay?" I didn't know his name, but it wasn't the first time I'd talked to him. And everyone in town knew I was married to the only remaining detective on the tiny Cadyville police force. His partner had transferred to the state crime lab a couple of months earlier, and they were still looking for a replacement.

I knelt and joined Meghan in unearthing the body. She was right: better safe than sorry. And she was right in thinking the foot belonged to a woman. The Timberland boot was about a size seven, the calf muscular but still feminine. Soon we revealed the other boot, then the pale bare skin of a knee, then the filthy hem of khaki hiking shorts. The compost was heavy and the pile rose at a steep angle. Organic steam rose from our efforts in tiny puffs. Meghan and I panted as the rich, coffee-colored earth rained back on our Sisyphean efforts to clear it.

My housemate paused in her digging to direct another resentful look at me, as if my bad habit of stumbling into fishy situations had somehow rubbed off on her. I ignored her, and she got back to work. Moments later, Tom joined us with two hand spades and a short shovel.

By the time the sirens approached, we had reached the bottom of a green T-shirt. There was little question left by then that the woman was most definitely dead.

TWO

HAVING DECLARED THE WOMAN beyond their help, the paramedics stood off to the side. Yellow *Police Do Not Cross* tape fluttered from tall stakes, marking off the area around the body. My husband, tall and angular, spoke with Tom Turner while the designated crime scene officers took pictures. The senior of the two, Officer Dawson, had started to lecture me about disturbing the scene until Sergeant Zahn stepped in to defend me. Apparently my husband's supervisor agreed it was better to make sure the victim wasn't slowly suffocating than to try and preserve evidence.

The thought made me shudder all over again.

But evidence of what? My mind flexed, reaching for possible explanations, each more fantastic than the last, and none of which felt the least bit viable. Could you accidentally be buried in a compost pile? I'd recently heard that part of a medical cadaver had turned up in the main recycling center in Seattle. But this was nothing like that.

Could there be a reasonable explanation?

Meghan and I stood on a small rise about a hundred feet away from the excitement. It gave us a good view of the goings on and, for now at least, the other CSA volunteers had left us alone. Meghan was a mess, mentally and physically, and I didn't look any better. We were both covered with dirt that had turned to patches of mud where we'd broken a sweat. It had matted into Meghan's dark curls, and no doubt I appeared more brunette than blonde myself. At least we'd used the hose to wash our faces and hands.

"Where's Erin?" Meghan's tone was urgent, and she craned her neck as if it would improve her eyesight. "I don't want her to see this."

The body was well-hidden, under a heavy tarp and behind a knot of police officers and firefighters. Still, I could see why Meghan would want to keep her twelve-year-old daughter away from the fray.

"I'll go look for her," I said, already scanning the farm for my youngest housemate, a miniature doppelganger of her mother, gray elf-eyes and all.

Barr nodded to Tom and his wife, Allie, then turned in our direction. When our eyes met, he lifted his chin in greeting and began making his way through the crowd to me. In the two years I'd known him, his chestnut hair had gained a bit more salt. Now it glinted in the sunlight. He wore cowboy boots and tan slacks with a cream-colored shirt augmented by one of his many string ties. Today an agate, polished and shaped into an oval, held the bolo at his throat.

He smiled and shook his head when he reached my side. "Looks like you've done it again."

"Nuh, uh. Meghan found her."

He shrugged. "Close enough."

I changed the subject before Meghan could work up another glare. "Have you seen Erin?"

"Nope. Has she gone missing?"

"What?" Meghan whirled toward us. "Why would you say that?"

Barr held up his hands. "Sorry. I'm sure she's around here."

"*So is a dead woman.*"

I gave him a look that said he deserved that. He ducked his head.

"Let's go ask the others." I put my arm around her shoulders and squeezed. Tension radiated off her. "Don't worry. We'll find her."

The crowd at the edge of the yellow tape parted as we approached. Dr. Jake Beagle loomed as close as he could get to the crime scene techs. His biceps strained at the fabric of his T-shirt, and he asked questions in a low, rumbling voice. I guessed his family medicine practice didn't often offer excitement like this, but at least he had a professional interest beyond the merely macabre.

Our long-time friend Bette, a potter, looked on with quiet horror, arms crossed and one hand cupped over her mouth as if to keep either inappropriate words or nausea at bay. She'd joined the CSA at our suggestion, and volunteered in the fields like we did. Tall and lean, Bette was deeply tanned from working outside and riding her one-speed bike all over town. Thick streaks of gray roped through her mane of long hair. Today, like most days, she wore it in a practical braid down her back like I'd worn mine before I'd felt compelled to cut my hair quite short. As always, her clothes were spattered with clay from her work.

Tom stood to one side; his wife, Allie, clutching his arm and leaning into him. He wore his usual farmer uniform of overalls and T-shirt, a look I thought he cultivated on purpose. Allie tended toward well-worn jeans, today topped with a loose, tie-dyed smock. She was short but wiry—far stronger than she looked—and uncharacteristic worry crinkled the skin around her mocha eyes.

Next to Allie, the Turners' full-time employee-apprentice, Nate Snow, shifted his weight from one foot to the other. He echoed Tom's overalled farmer look, only his dark hair was pulled back into a ponytail and topped with a battered cap with the Everett AquaSox frog logo. His ice-blue eyes were hidden behind a pair of Oakleys that had seen better days.

On the other side of him Allie's sister, Hallie, pressed brightly glossed lips together and frowned at the figure on the ground. She looked as different from Allie as an identical twin could, with her heavy eye makeup and a designer silk shirt that had no business anywhere near a farm. Nate patted her arm, but she jerked away from his touch. Daphne Sparks, a tall, pale horticulture student I'd first met when her roommate had been strangled, walked up behind Nate and laid her hand on his shoulder. He slid his arm around her waist, earning a hard look from Hallie. She sidled to her right to stand away from them.

"Anyone seen Erin Bly?" Barr asked, taking charge now that he'd panicked Meghan.

Blank looks met his question.

"Erin!" Meghan called. "*Erin*!"

Jake Beagle and Daphne joined in, calling Erin's name. But there was no response.

"She's probably with Clarissa," Allie Turner said, blinking rapidly.

"And where's Clarissa?" I asked.

Allie shrugged. Given her dazed expression I wondered if she might be suffering from mild shock.

Meghan stared at her. She always knew where her daughter was, or at least where she was supposed to be. And right now she was supposed to be close by. As it was, my friend didn't like how much time her daughter had been spending with the Turner girl. Though only one year older, Clarissa tried to act like a sixteen-year-old—makeup, clothes modeled on sexy pop stars, and an interest in boys that went alarmingly beyond her years.

"About an hour ago I saw them walking toward the main road," Nate offered. "Looked like they were heading downtown."

The Turner Farm was on the outskirts of Cadyville, just inside the city limits. That's why the police rather than the sheriff's department were handling the woman in the compost pile. It was only a couple miles to First Street on the wide, paved road that wound by the farm, but there wasn't a sidewalk. Besides, Erin hadn't asked permission to leave.

I cringed and turned toward our housemate. "Now, Meghan, don't worry. I'll jump in the Rover and go get her. I'm sure I can find her."

Her nostrils flared. "No. I'll go. Little miss and I need to have a talk."

Uh oh. I silently wished Erin good luck. "Okay."

She began marching toward the small gravel parking lot.

"Call me when you find her," I called.

She raised her hand in a gesture of frustration and dismissal, neither of which were aimed at us.

Barr watched her go. "Let me know if you don't hear from her soon. I don't like the idea of Erin running around on her own like that."

"All right, but I'm sure she's fine. I happen to know she's working her mother hard for a cell phone. Doing something like this might get her one so Meghan will always be able to track her down."

"Oh, that's devious," he said. "Do you really think she'd . . . ? Never mind. That kid is too smart for her own good."

"No, she's too smart for our own good. Sure you want your very own?"

His eyes softened. "I still do if you do."

"How long do you think you'll have to work tonight?" It sounded like I was changing the subject, but I wasn't.

"Zahn said something about an all-nighter, but I think I can talk him out of that at least. He's very enthusiastic about stepping in since Robin left." Referring to Detective Robin Lane, his erstwhile partner who'd up and transferred. She was smart, which was a gain for the crime lab, but tactless, so working away from the public was good, too. It was a win for everyone except the Cadyville Police Department and my husband's workload.

"The main problem right now is we don't know who she is." Barr gestured toward the tarp with his chin.

"No identification?"

"Nothing in her pockets at all."

I tugged on Barr's sleeve, and we moved away from the group. "Shoot," I whispered. "I was hoping you wouldn't have to work *that* late."

He laughed. "Well, you're the one who called this in."

I scowled.

"What's wrong?" he said. And he wasn't talking about the wrongness of a dead body laying seventy-five feet away from us.

I pulled the thermometer out of my pocket. When he saw it he raised his eyebrows.

"Is it time?"

"Maybe."

"I thought the whole idea was to be precise about the best time for conception."

"Keep your voice down! You have to keep records for a while. At least I think so."

"That's vague."

"Hey, I'm new at this! Would it be so bad to try tonight?"

He kissed me on the forehead, which was pretty daring considering how dirty I still was. "Don't be daft. Maybe you should wait up for me after all."

I harrumphed but felt better.

A woman's voice snagged our attention. "Don't be ridiculous! I've seen plenty of dead people. Let me take a look."

I peered around Barr. Sergeant Zahn had his hand on the arm of my favorite septuagenarian and spinning mentor, Ruth Black. Yesterday she'd mentioned coming by the farm with a few of her favorite canning recipes for the CSA members—I wanted the one for pickled beets in particular. I hadn't even noticed when she'd pulled her ancient, mint-green Buick into the parking lot.

Now she shrugged off the sergeant's hand, ducked under the yellow tape and stood next to the body, her recipe cards still clutched in one hand. Her short white hair spiked around her head in a furry halo.

Zahn followed close on her heels. "That's fine ma'am, but we can't have you disturbing anything."

Ruth bristled. "Even I can tell the whole area has already been disturbed. Now do you, or do you not, know who that poor thing is?"

"Not yet, ma'am." The muscles worked along Zahn's jaw, but he managed to work up a smile.

"I know a lot of people in this town, Sergeant, so I might be able to tell you. Just let me get a good look at her face."

He sighed and glanced over at Barr. My husband went and joined them inside the tape, and I moved to stand between Hallie and Daphne. My husband positioned himself next to Zahn to effectively shield the tarp from onlookers' curious eyes. He stooped and his arm moved, presumably pulling it back a few inches.

A long silence ensued before Ruth said, "No, I don't think I've ever seen her before. I don't believe she's from around here." She gazed down. "Poor darling. She's not very old, is she?"

Barr murmured something and his arm moved again. He stood up. A somber Ruth trudged back to our group. Sidling up next to me, she leaned close. "I wish I could have helped."

I put my arm around her shoulders and squeezed. "It's okay. Thanks for trying."

Dr. Beagle called out, "Is there anything I can do, Sarge?"

Sarge? Oh, my. Zahn had to love that. I looked at Barr, who had pasted on a perfectly neutral expression. His poker face was so much better than mine. I turned away so the sergeant wouldn't see the grin tugging at my lips. Exchanging glances with Ruth, I saw my amusement echoed in her eyes.

"I think we have everything under control, Doctor," Zahn said. "The medical examiner's office will be here soon. He'll be able to determine cause of death."

"Could it be an accident?" I asked. Hoping.

Despite everyone's assumption that I liked being involved in murder cases, I really didn't. I just felt like sometimes I had to step in because other people couldn't. Or wouldn't. So I wanted this to be an innocent death—horrible as it was. I looked at the shrouded figure, so recently covered with compost as if she were a bone buried by a giant dog.

Barr caught my eye and shook his head slowly. "I don't think so. Looks like she was hit in the head."

"That could still be an accident," I insisted.

But deep down, I knew better.

THREE

My cell phone rang as they were loading the body into the morgue van. "I found Erin," Meghan said. "She's fine."

"Where was she?"

"Eating ice cream. Listen, I'll see you at home, okay?"

Which meant she wanted to unload but not in front of her daughter.

"You bet. I'm going to finish the tomatoes, and then I'll be there."

We said our goodbyes as the van drove away, smoothly accelerating once it hit pavement. I watched until it was out of sight, then turned and strode into the greenhouse. The sound of doors slamming in the parking lot drifted through the opaque plastic. There were still tomato vines trailing on the ground, and I had time to finish the job before I needed to be back at the house to pack up the waiting wholesale orders for my Winding Road handmade soap and bath products.

Oh, right. Who was I trying to fool? Barr was up at the main house, talking with Tom and Allie Turner. Hallie lived with them, and Nate Snow lived in the cutest vintage Airstream trailer in back of the farmhouse. If anyone knew the dead woman, you'd think it would be someone who lived on the property where she was found. My reluctance to get involved notwithstanding, I was curious enough to want to know who the owner of the Timberland boots had been.

I'd finished with the tomatoes and was returning the remaining strips of soft cloth and a pair of clippers to the tool shed when Barr and Sergeant Zahn approached. The latter frowned down at the ground as he walked. My husband's expression was outwardly placid, though I recognized the tightness around his eyes. They stopped in front of me and Zahn raised his head, scanning my face for a few seconds before saying, "So. You found another one."

I shook my head emphatically. "Meghan Bly found her. You remember Meghan, don't you?"

He nodded. "Good friend of yours."

"Yes. Barr and I have a little apartment on the upper level of her house."

"The same house where you make your soap."

With a lopsided grimace, I sighed. The first time I'd ever met him had been in my basement workroom, a dead body at our feet. It had been the first time I'd met Barr, too, so something good had come out of it. Come to think of it, a lot of good had come out of those sad circumstances, including my friendship with Tootie Hanover and the eventual good riddance of Meghan's slimy ex.

I suddenly wished Tootie hadn't taken off on an Alaskan cruise with her boyfriend. Aren't ninety-somethings supposed to stick closer to home? It was hard to complain about her and Felix having fun, though. They'd certainly earned it. But they sure had bad timing. This was exactly the kind of situation that drove me to Tootie for advice.

"Where were you when Ms. Bly found this body?" Zahn asked.

I gestured with my chin. "In the distribution shed. Any idea how long she's been there?"

"We won't know for sure until the M.E. gets back to us," Zahn said. "Do you have any ideas?"

I shot a glance at Barr, who blinked back at me. No help there. I regarded Zahn with suspicion. Since when did he ask my advice about anything? He'd always been kind of snotty about my involvement in anything remotely resembling a police matter. But now he waited for me to speak with an expression of apparent interest.

"Well," I began, ready for his interest to turn to ire. "She was pretty well buried except for her foot. The Turners let their pigs out to root through the compost regularly, though, and I saw a couple of them working that edge of the pile earlier today." I swallowed, remembering that pigs will eat almost anything. In fact, hadn't some serial killer fed his victims to his hogs? Or maybe that was just an urban—or rather rural—myth.

I hoped so. Ick.

He nodded, slowly. "Ms. Black insisted on looking at the body."

"Hmm. I saw that. Ruth isn't fazed by much."

"She said she didn't think the woman was from around here."

"Well, if anyone would know, she would."

"Would you be willing to take a look? See if you recognize her?"

Barr's head swiveled toward his superior. "Sergeant, I don't think—"

Zahn held up his hand. "Of course. Sophie Mae doesn't need to look at the actual body. But we should have a decent picture by tomorrow morning."

"Okay," I said. If Ruth could look at the body, I could manage a picture. At least I thought I could. After all, I'd already seen three dead bodies up close and personal. In situ, if you will. None of them had been pre-buried, though.

Barr said, "We'll be able to show it to everyone associated with the farm, then."

Again with the slow nod from Zahn. "Naturally. But I'm especially interested in what your wife has to say."

"Why?" Barr's response was blunt.

The sergeant smiled. "Because Sophie Mae has a knack for finding killers. Wouldn't you agree?"

"Uh..."

"And wouldn't you agree that being down one detective, we can use all the help we can get?"

"Uh..." I was surprised to see Barr at a loss for words.

At least I wasn't. "Don't be ridiculous. Of course I'll take a look at that unfortunate woman's picture, just like everyone else. But I'm not getting involved in any police work. That's all done and over with, Sergeant."

His response consisted of a small sound in the back of his throat and a slow blink of skepticism.

"It just wouldn't be right," I insisted. "After all, I'm going to be a mother!"

His eyebrows shot up at that.

Almost as far as Barr's did.

"And then I had to backpedal and explain that I'm not actually pregnant yet," I told Meghan. "I thought Barr was going to die. I'm pretty sure he hadn't shared anything about our baby plans with his boss."

"Good heavens, Sophie Mae. Why would he?" Her clean hair was still damp, and she wore white shorts and a skimpy pink tank to show off her tan. When you managed to get a tan in the Pacific Northwest, you showed it off. She seemed to have reclaimed some of her Zen, too.

I'd come home later than I'd planned. Putting off the Winding Road orders, I showered away the muck and donned a light cotton skirt, T-shirt, and flip flops. Now we were in the kitchen cutting up tomatoes, eggplant, peppers, zucchini, and onions for ratatouille. A whole chicken soaked in orange juice brine on the butcher block table, soon to go onto the barbecue's rotisserie. A pot of orzo roiled on the stove for pasta salad. A fragrant bouquet of herbs lay on the cutting board, ready to be chopped and added to the salad, along with homemade feta, scallions, and carrots.

The door to Erin's room was pointedly closed.

I got out the grater and started on the carrots while Meghan smashed a few heads of garlic and tossed them in a Dutch oven with the onions and peppers. She ignited the burner under the stew pot and drizzled olive oil and a bit of kosher salt over the vegetables. Soon the pungent aroma of sautéing garlic filled the room. I breathed it in, reminding myself this was the kind of simple moment that made me grateful to be alive.

"No reason," I said. "I wouldn't have said anything if Zahn hadn't been pushing me to help."

"I'm glad you said no." Her voice was soft but decisive. Meghan liked things nice and predictable. Sometimes being my best friend was a little hard on her.

After a few minutes I ventured, "Where did you find Erin and Clarissa?"

She made a pffft sound. "In the Pie Shop. Erin said they started taking a walk and ended up all the way in town, but Clarissa came right out and said they were meeting a couple of boys for ice cream."

"Any sign of the boys?"

"Nope. Maybe she was making it up. Or maybe they were late."

"I don't suppose Erin suggested that if she had her own cell phone you could have been in contact."

Meghan's eye's narrowed. "Funny you should mention that. How did you know?"

"I didn't, not for sure. What did you tell her?"

"That I'd think about it." Our eyes met, and I saw barely contained fury in hers.

I let out a whoosh of air. "Boy, this has been one crappy day for you, hasn't it?"

She held her combative stance for a few moments longer, then her shoulders slumped, and she nodded. "Monumentally." Given her usual determination to be upbeat, that was a huge admission.

"Is Kelly coming over for dinner?"

My housemate shrugged as if there were a lot more than spaghetti straps on her shoulders.

"How 'bout I call him?" I asked.

A moment of hesitation, then a nod. "But I'll call. He should know what he's getting into." Then a small smile.

Which I returned. "I don't think he'll mind if you're in a bad mood. He's pretty smitten, after all."

Her expression softened. "Yeah."

So smitten, in fact, that Kelly O'Connell had moved his private investigation firm—can one man claim to be a firm?—all the way to Cadyville from New Jersey to be with Meghan. They'd done the long-distance relationship thing for over a year, and I was glad to see things progress.

I'd lived with Meghan and Erin Bly for five years before meeting Barr. Then I'd lived with them when we were courting, and after Barr and I got married we'd renovated Meghan's house so that we had a little apartment upstairs to ourselves. Still, Barr and I spent a lot of time in the main areas of the house. I ran Winding Road Bath Products out of the basement, and Meghan practiced massage therapy in the former front parlor of the big Victorian.

The Bly girls were precious to me, and I wanted the very best for them both. Kelly O'Connell was a good guy. Meghan deserved a good guy after her disastrous marriage to Erin's father. He didn't even send child support anymore, and she'd stopped trying to get it, considering it a small price to pay to have him out of their lives. Kelly was smart, stable, possessed a kind of rugged handsomeness, and was devoted to my friend.

It was about time.

Meghan went out to the entryway, and I heard the melodious beeping of the phone as she punched in the numbers. Soon her murmurs drifted from her client waiting room where she'd sought out a little privacy. I finished with the carrots, drained and rinsed the pasta with cold water, and chopped the herbs to go into the salad. I stirred chunks of zucchini, eggplant, and tomato, along with more olive oil and salt, into the ratatouille and popped it all into the oven to stew for a couple hours. Then I wiped my hands on a towel and went down the hallway to Erin's bedroom.

The closed door gave me pause. It was unusual, and definitely contained a message. A message I decided to ignore. I knocked lightly on the wood.

FOUR

"Go away." Erin's voice was faint but firm.

"Erin?"

A few beats of quiet, then her voice came again, louder this time. She'd moved closer. "Sophie Mae?"

"Yeah. Can I come in?"

After several moments the door opened a crack. One gray eye peered at me through the opening. "Did she send you to talk to me?"

"If you mean your mother, nope."

The eye blinked, bright with the thoughts that swirled in her precocious mind. Then she stepped back and opened the door. I walked into her bedroom, and the latch snicked closed behind me as she shut it again. At the foot of the bed Brodie, Erin's Pembroke Welsh corgi, raised his graying muzzle. He sniffed a few times, decided I didn't have anything interesting to eat and went back to sleep. On the desk I spied the leather-bound, blank book I'd given Erin for her birthday in May. All summer she'd filled the pages with her fantasy novel. Needless to say, I was anxious to read it when it was finished.

If it was finished. Her attention did tend to drift from one interest to another.

Crossing my arms across my chest and leaning against the wall next to her overflowing bookcase, I considered her. She was practically my adopted daughter, since I'd lived with them since she was five. Still, I wasn't her mother, and right now that seemed like a good thing. Not because I didn't love her to death, but because—at the moment at least—I wasn't "the enemy."

Dark curls now grown down to her shoulders framed almond-shaped eyes, a slightly turned-up nose and pixie-bow lips which often opened into a wide grin. She wasn't grinning now, though. Suspicion lingered in her gaze as she sat down on the bed, her slight frame barely disturbing the log cabin quilt covering it. A smudge of glittery eye shadow and pink spots of blush on her cheeks betrayed part of her activities with Clarissa Turner that afternoon.

Looking beyond the makeup remnants, I realized with a shock that Erin Bly was going to be a stunningly beautiful woman. Given how she took after her mother, that shouldn't have surprised me. And Meghan was a clever bear, too, but Erin had something else going on, a liveliness that danced behind her pupils and a sharper wit that was beginning to manifest as she got older. It would make her a formidable adult.

A formidable teenager, too. I managed to contain my sigh at the thought.

"So how come you took off without telling anyone?" I asked in a casual tone.

"I don't know why everyone's making such a big deal about it." Her lower lip crept out.

I grinned at her. "Really?"

"Yeah!"

Raising my eyebrows, I waited.

Her nostrils flared, and she tried to stare me down. I blinked and waited, knowing full well that she understood why her mother had been so upset. Finally her gaze dropped to the floor, and one shoulder bobbed up and down in a half shrug.

"I didn't want to worry anyone, but I'm not a little kid anymore." Her chin rose in defiance. "I'm twelve, Sophie Mae! I shouldn't have to ask permission for every little thing."

"If I'd left, I would have told someone," I said. "And I'm thirty-eight."

"Yeah. Well."

"You get why your mom kind of freaked out."

She got up and looked out the window at the urban chicken coop in the backyard. "Yeah, I guess so." Turning back, she put her hands on her hips. "But she didn't have to embarrass me like that."

"What did she do?"

"Came barreling into the Pie Shop looking like Pig Pen—worse even—and started yelling. Clarissa must think she's nuts."

I doubted that Meghan gave a hoot what Miss Clarissa thought.

"We tried to explain, but she wouldn't listen."

"You were meeting some boys downtown?"

"No! Well, maybe Clarissa planned to, but I didn't know anything about it. I just wanted to get some ice cream."

"Hmm. And maybe con your mom into getting you a cell phone by presenting her with a practical situation where it would have been useful?"

She stared at me like a startled rabbit, then a you-caught-me grin tugged at the corner of her mouth. She scowled it down. "That's just weird, Sophie Mae."

"Uh, huh. At any rate, it sounds like a whole pile of miscommunication. Maybe you should apologize to your mom."

"What for? I didn't do anything wrong."

"Yes, you did. And so did Clarissa. And you know it."

She glared at me.

"You know I'm right. And your mom is having a pretty crappy day. Did she tell you what happened at the farm?"

Erin shook her head.

"She found a body in the compost pile." I figured Erin was going to find out anyway, and she'd handled our previous run-ins with mayhem pretty well.

Curiosity replaced her ire. "Like … a person?"

Slowly, I nodded my head.

Her jaw dropped. "You're kidding!"

"Nope. So lighten up and come help with dinner. Barr's working tonight, but I think Kelly's coming over." Her mother's boyfriend had become one of Erin's favorite people since he moved to Cadyville.

She pressed her lips together, thinking. "Okay."

I opened her bedroom door, and she followed me down the hallway. Brodie jumped down from the bed and followed, his toenails clicking on the hardwood floor. Upon entering the kitchen the first words out of Erin's mouth were, "So was the dead person a man or a woman?"

Meghan whirled from where she was working at the counter, her eyes widening at me in a silent question.

"I figured it wasn't exactly a secret." I almost managed to keep the defensiveness out of my voice.

The front door opened, and a voice called out, "Hello! Anyone home?" Thank goodness, Kelly had arrived just in time to distract my friend from my child-rearing faux pas.

"In here," we chorused.

Moments later he came around the corner, stopping in the open doorway. He was a couple inches taller than my five-foot-six, and olive skin tanned darker by the summer sun stretched over high cheekbones. His dark hair and eyes reflected a tribal bloodline in his genealogy, and his full lips parted in a smile when he saw Meghan. He stepped in and swooped her into a big hug.

"You okay?" he murmured into her hair.

Silent, she nodded against his shoulder. Erin and I exchanged a glance.

"Come on," I said. "You can get today's eggs while I pull a few more scallions for the salad."

As we left I heard Kelly say, "So how is it you found her instead of Sophie Mae?"

According to their CSA pamphlet, Tom and Allie Turner had moved to Cadyville with a dream of starting a farm that would produce enough vegetables to feed 100 families for the summer. Members paid a flat fee and shared in the harvest—and risks—of the organic farm. The growing season in the Pacific Northwest is pretty long and frosts are light, so "summer" turns out to be about half the year if you grow the right things—with a cold frame and a little luck with the weather you can grow some kind of fresh vegetable almost year-round. The frequent rains were the worst problem, promoting powdery mildew and even rotting root vegetables left in the ground. But Tom had grown up on a farm in the area and knew what he was doing. Allie was no slouch either. Eventually they hoped to offer fresh vegetables year-round.

For an additional fee their farm members could get eggs each week, and plans were in the works to offer pasture-raised poultry and pork in the next few years. Since our backyard hens provided enough eggs for us and a couple of neighbors, we didn't need the Turners' eggs, and in truth we had four small raised beds where we had grown our own vegetables for years. But while we had a few plants of this and that, we couldn't grow enough of most things to put up for the winter in addition to providing our daily needs. We had already been investigating a local pea patch to augment our growing space in May when one of my teenaged employees, Cyan Waters, met Allie Turner at the Thursday night Farmers Market in downtown Cadyville. She was selling Winding Road Bath Products, and Allie was selling the first of the vegetables from the farm.

Meghan and I had found the solution to our problem. We worked on the farm about the same amount of time we would have put in on a pea-patch garden and paid half the amount of non-working CSA members while netting more variety and abundance than we ever could have produced on our own. Plus, Tom and Allie allowed us to buy overages and seconds at a steep discount. Between the big freezer now sitting in the corner of my basement workroom and the pantry off the kitchen already beginning to fill with home-canned tomato products, pickles, and fruit, we would have enough tasty goodness to last until it would be time to start putting up the gardens all over again.

Eggs and scallions in hand, Erin and I returned to the kitchen. Kelly sat at the butcher block table sipping a nut brown ale, Meghan across from him with what I guessed was a much-needed glass of white wine.

He looked up when we came in. "Hey, you two. You ran out before I could say hello."

"You seemed kind of busy," Erin said.

He laughed and even Meghan smiled. She put her arm out in invitation to her daughter and raised her eyebrows.

Erin hesitated, then moved into her embrace. "I'm still mad at you."

Her mother gave her a squeeze. "That's okay. I'm still mad at you, too."

"Well, I'm glad that's settled," I said, pouring a finger of Laphroaig into the bottom of a jelly jar and taking a sip. It wended its way down my throat, smoke and fire, and I sighed.

Kelly leaned his elbow on the table and propped his chin on his palm. "Meghan told me they don't know who the woman is."

The "woman." Not the "dead woman." I glanced at Erin. She'd stilled, willing herself invisible so we'd talk in front of her.

"I'm sure they'll figure it out." I opened a kitchen drawer, removed a long-handled lighter and held it out to Kelly. "You're practically family now. Why don't you go start the grill?"

FIVE

Opening all the basement windows to the evening, I breathed in the rapidly cooling air as the sun approached the horizon. This had been my workspace ever since I started Winding Road Bath Products with a simple line of homemade, cold-processed soap. After my first husband, Mike Reynolds, died, Meghan had invited me to come live with her in Cadyville. Only after she'd asked had I realized how much I needed companionship. Lord knew she was not only one of my favorite people in the world, but we had a history of living together in circumstances far less ideal than her Victorian-style house. We'd been roommates at the University of Washington for four years.

So I'd quit my mid-level administrative position in the Lake Washington School District and moved thirty miles north, taking a job in a small bookstore. After Winding Road took off, I was able to quit and devote all of my time to my very own business. It was a lot of work, and always more of a risk than holding out my hand for a paycheck come Friday, but it was worth it. I loved being my own boss, working at home, and having flexibility in my schedule.

Of course that meant long hours, especially in the early years. Now late nights had become rarer. Since Barr was still at the cop shop tonight, I'd planned to pack up the orders for UPS after dinner, but when I came downstairs I discovered that my uber-efficient helpers, Cyan and Kalie, had already done most of the work. I finished up, set the boxes by the back door to put out in the morning, and considered what else I could accomplish that evening.

It looked like some basic soap making was in order.

I donned a long white apron and placed rubber gloves and a pair of dorky chemistry goggles on the central work island. The radio on the counter by the stove played Emmylou Harris at low volume as I measured oils into a large pot and set a low flame under them. Then I donned the gloves and goggles and weighed out a portion of sodium hydroxide crystals—good, old-fashioned lye. When I added water to the lye in the big bowl attached to the industrial bread mixer, it reacted by chemically heating the liquid. A drift of unpleasant-smelling steam curled up, and I backed to the stove to check the temperature of the oils. I opened a bottle of basil essential oil and inhaled the spicy licorice scent, wiping away all traces of the hot lye.

While the oils had to heat up, the lye had to cool down. For the basic lavender-and-basil scented soap I was making this evening, I wanted the oils at 100° and the lye at 85° when I poured the oils into the mixer. There the beaters would combine them thoroughly, and the process of saponification would begin.

"You look like a mad scientist."

I whirled to find Kelly standing at the bottom of the narrow staircase leading down from the kitchen.

"Can I come in?"

"Sure." I waved him over and stripped off the gloves and goggles.

He slid onto a stool at the end of the island and quirked an eyebrow. "Is all that really necessary?"

"The safety equipment? Not everyone uses it, but I have two young employees. I want them to be safe, and it doesn't hurt for me to follow the same rules."

"You are careful, aren't you." Something in the way he said that held significance beyond handling dangerous chemicals.

I cocked my head to one side and waited.

"I'm only saying you aren't exactly... reckless."

"What's that supposed to mean?" I tried not to bristle as I remembered a few times I'd been more reckless than I should have. Sneaking out to see who was in the car watching our house. Searching a stranger's house for murder evidence. Even stealing Meghan's keys so I could go through a dead man's office, looking for a murder motive. But truthfully, most of the times I'd been in real danger hadn't been a result of my recklessness, but of being in the wrong place at the wrong time.

So maybe Kelly was right.

Except I'd been in those wrong places because of my own curiosity. Kind of made one ponder the fate of certain cats.

"I mean you aren't stupid," he said.

"Gee, thanks."

He held up his palms. “Aren’t you wondering about the woman you and Meghan found in the compost pile today?”

“Of course I am.”

“But not enough to do anything about it.”

Crossing my arms over my chest, I narrowed my eyes. “My husband is a police detective. I hardly think he needs my help.”

“Doesn’t sound like that’s true. In fact, from what Meghan told me, it sounds like his boss is interested in having you help.”

“Listen, I know you love detecting,” I said. “It’s what you do for a living, and from what I understand, you’re pretty good at it. Maybe you should help the police, if you’re so sure they need it.”

He shook his head. “I couldn’t do what you can do. You know people in this community, Sophie Mae. You can talk to them and get them to talk to you.”

“What’s the matter with you? Isn’t it clear that I don’t want to do that anymore?”

“I don’t believe you.”

I took a deep breath, stirred the pot on the stove and tested the temperature. Almost ninety degrees.

“Barr and I want to have a baby. I can’t go gallivanting around, poking my nose into other people’s business if I have a baby.”

His lips turned up. “Ah. That’s different than not wanting to get involved. That’s you not being reckless.”

I threw up my hands. “Okay. Have it your way. You’re right. I’m a fuddy duddy. Some people call that being responsible.”

“Are you pregnant?”

I stared at him. “What? No. Not yet.” Not that it was any of his business, really.

"So if you were to help discover the identity of the dead woman buried under several feet of dirt, you wouldn't be harming your child."

"But, Kelly—"

"Your not-even-conceived child."

"You are such a, such a ... *man*!"

He laughed. "I hope so." He slid off the stool and strode to the stairs. Turned back and met my eye. "You have a natural talent for finding things out. If I had an agency, I'd hire you in a heartbeat. You're good at tracking down the truth, and you do it for the best reason—you want to help people."

I felt the skin tighten across my face in reaction to his words.

"And face it, Sophie Mae—you enjoy it, too. Plenty of private investigators are also parents."

He turned to go up the stairs.

"Does Meghan know you're down here?"

Over his shoulder he said, "She's playing Clue with Erin. I need to get back."

I listened to his footsteps clump up to the kitchen, and the door opened and shut. Dang it. Meghan would throw a fit if she knew her beau was encouraging me. Still, I had to admit I was flattered that someone who investigated crime professionally thought I had a talent for it.

And he was right. I had enjoyed being involved in Barr's cases—as well as a couple of deaths that would have slipped under the radar as either suicide or accident if I hadn't followed up on my gut feelings. Figuring out whodunit was satisfying, though the process was often frustrating. But it appealed to my sense of justice, making things tidy in the world.

I loved my life. It was full and satisfying, and only seemed to be getting better and better. And part of that was because it had been occasionally punctuated by the excitement of a murder investigation. But I could still get that vicariously through Barr, right?

Maybe.

Besides, if Barr didn't get some help, he'd be working so many hours there wouldn't be any time at all for making babies.

I sighed and took the temperature of the lye, then pulled the thermometer out of my pocket and took my own.

98.1°.

SIX

A LIGHT WIND RUSTLED the maple leaves outside the open bedroom window, a constant shushing that would have normally lulled me right to sleep. The temperature had dropped so the room was cool, but I was snug under the quilt.

Snug and alone.

Barr had called around ten o'clock to let me know he'd still be a few more hours. By that time I'd poured the lavender-basil soap into molds to harden and cleaned up the workroom. Upstairs I stopped by Erin's bedroom to find she'd fallen asleep with one arm draped around a snoozing Brodie. I turned off her light and moved on to the living room where Meghan and Kelly were watching a movie. One look at them cuddled together on the sofa told me they'd appreciate a little privacy, so I'd gone up to our digs to wait for my hubby.

After a few minutes watching television in our little sitting room, it became apparent not even the Food Network could hold my attention. So I sat at the bistro table in our shiny kitchenette and doodled ideas for new Winding Road products. I already had soaps and milk bath, bath salts, and melts and teas. Lip balms and lotion bars were mainstays, as were foot scrub, facial cleanser, and air fresheners. At this point adding new items could only increase sales. Maybe a line of herbal salves? Or perhaps an assortment of fragrant body oils—effective and cost efficient with the added benefit of aromatherapy. I could attest to that because I already made several types for my personal use, as well as providing Meghan with custom blends for her massage clients.

Okay, body oils it would be. I'd order the raw materials in the morning.

That decided, I stood and stretched, glancing at the clock on the microwave. Almost midnight. Usually I'd have been in bed at least an hour ago, Barr or no Barr. Tonight I wanted to know whether they'd identified the compost lady, as I thought of her somewhat embarrassingly. But there was no telling how late my husband would be.

Enough. I had to get some sleep.

So I changed into my jammies, crawled between the sheets, and turned the lamp on Barr's nightstand to low.

I should have known as soon as I shut my eyes the image of a dirty green-and-blue striped sock would fill my mental movie screen. I'd been doing my best to distract myself all evening, but now it was just me, the shushing wind, and that damn sock.

After fifteen minutes, I switched on my light and opened the suspense novel I'd been gradually working through. Better to read about fictional serial killers than think about real-life dead bodies.

The door to the stairs at the end of the hall was open so I could hear the front door. At a little after one it opened and closed. Moments later footsteps sounded on the stairs, then quieted on the carpet. I stuck a bookmark right in the middle of a steamy love scene and waited.

Barr came into the bedroom, tugging at his tie. "Oh, hon." He stopped and looked down at me apologetically. "I didn't really mean for you to stay awake. I'm exhausted, not quite up for—"

"Like I could have slept. Don't worry—I'm not exactly in a sexy mood, either. Have you eaten?"

He shook his head. "Didn't have time."

I threw back the covers and slipped on my ducky slippers. "There's some leftover chicken downstairs."

"I don't want to wake anyone," he said, sinking onto the bed and pulling off one cowboy boot and then the other.

"How about a quick grilled cheese?"

His smile was tired. "Sure. Thanks."

I bustled down to the kitchenette, flipped on the overhead light and got out a cast-iron pan. I buttered two pieces of Meghan's homemade bread and began slicing sharp cheddar. Barr joined me, wearing a pair of worn flannel pajama pants that were a whole lot more attractive than they sound. Doing my best to ignore the impure thoughts my tired husband's bare chest aroused, I dug around in the half-sized fridge, found some ham, and added a few thin slices to the sandwich. Once it was sizzling in the pan and the smell of browning bread filled the small space, I sat down across from him.

"So?"

He took a deep breath. "Well, there'll be a full autopsy later. But she was definitely hit on the head with the proverbial blunt instrument a couple days ago. Probably a shovel. She was killed in the last twelve to thirty-six hours. The heat in the compost pile kind of fudged up the time of death, so that's as close as the M.E. could get. Unfortunately, that means alibis will be almost impossible to identify or track."

I winced. "So you're investigating it as a homicide."

"Absolutely." He grimaced. Opened his mouth to say something, then closed it.

"What?" I asked.

He shook his head.

I knew enough to let it go … and circle back later. "Did you find out who she is … was?"

"No idea. They took her fingerprints, but running them takes a while, and she'd have to be in the system already for there to be a match. I won't say it's impossible to identify her that way, but it might be a long shot. We did get a pretty decent picture, though."

I perked up at that. Getting up to flip his sandwich, I asked, "Do you have it?"

"Hang on a sec."

By the time he returned from the bedroom, his sandwich was oozing cheese onto a plate. I added a few potato chips, silently asked the local food gods' forgiveness, poured a tall glass of iced herbal tea, and put his late dinner in front of him. He handed me the eight-by-ten photo, face down, and dug in.

Sinking into the chair opposite, I fingered the thick glossy paper without turning it over. It was quite possible I was about to look at the picture of someone I knew, or at least someone I'd met. I inhaled, braced, and flipped it over.

The photo had a kind of sepia quality, as if it weren't really in color but not black-and-white, either. But instead of sepia browns it was in varying shades of blue and gray. Must have been a result of the light in the morgue where the picture had been taken. I had to admit the thought kind of gave me the heebie-jeebies.

The mystery woman was shown from her bare shoulders up. Strands of short, mouse-brown hair escaped in a dirty halo around her face. Her neck was slender, her skin unlined and very pale. Well, duh. It would be, wouldn't it? High cheekbones and a heart-shaped face revealed classic bone structure. Even in repose, she was stunning.

"Sorry," I said. "I've never seen her before."

Barr swallowed and wiped his mouth with a napkin. He'd already snarfed half the sandwich. "I'm not surprised. If you'd known her, I would have expected Ruth Black to, as well. Tom and Allie Turner didn't recognize her, either."

"Who all did you show it to?"

"The Turners, Jake Beagle's wife—"

"Felicia," I said.

He nodded. "And Bette Anders down the street. After that it was just too late."

"What about Nate Snow and dear little Clarissa?"

"It was after nine by the time I got out there. I think I woke the Turners up."

"I bet you did. They're farmers, after all. Early risers by definition."

"Tom said Nate went to see a movie in Monroe with his girlfriend, and Clarissa was already asleep. At least that's what they said. I doubt they wanted her to see it."

"Probably not. What about Hallie?"

"She was out, too. Tom didn't know where." He took a sip of iced tea. "Allie gave me a list of all the CSA members. There are more than I thought."

"Do I detect a note of frustration?"

"It's a ton of legwork. I don't want to offload it onto patrol, though." He shrugged and shoved the last of the sandwich in his mouth.

I leaned my elbow on the table and rested my chin on my palm. "Does Sergeant Zahn really want my help?"

Barr eyed me, slowly chewing.

"More importantly, do you want my help?"

He swallowed and took a final swig of iced tea. Then he put out his hand parallel to the table and made a waffle-y back-and-forth gesture. "I'm ambivalent. I do like it when you're involved in my work, and I know you're good at finding things out."

I thought of Kelly telling me the same thing and tried not to preen.

"But on the other hand, it can be dangerous. I don't like that."

"What you do every day is dangerous. I don't stop you."

"Sophie Mae, it's my job."

"Which you *chose*. You know you could do something else if you wanted to."

He opened his mouth. Closed it again.

"I'll be careful," I said.

"You always say that."

"And I always mean it."

"But you have a point," he said. "You're a grown woman. I can't tell you what to do. Besides, your moxie is one of the reasons I fell in love with you."

"Oh, you silver-tongued devil." I leaned across the table and kissed him. His lips tasted of honey-cured ham. "Do you want another sandwich?"

He shook his head. "Nah. It'll be hard enough to sleep as it is."

"I doubt that." I rose and rinsed his dishes in the sink while he went in the bathroom to brush his teeth.

Flipping off the light switch, I shuffled down to our bedroom. He'd tumbled into bed and now reached for his light.

I crawled in beside him. "Barr?"

"Hmm?"

"You were going to tell me something else earlier. Something about why you're investigating this as a homicide. She was hit in the head, right?"

There was a long silence, and I thought he'd gone to sleep. Then he cleared his throat and said, "Yes. But blunt force trauma wasn't the cause of death."

My forehead wrinkled. "Then what was?"

After a long moment he opened his eyes and looked at me in the dim light. "Suffocation."

It took me a few moments to get it. Stunned, I sat up in bed. "She was *buried alive*?"

He exhaled and nodded. "We'll know for sure after the full autopsy. But, yeah. It sure looks like it."

SEVEN

SURE ENOUGH, MY DEAR husband drifted off in no time. But if thinking about the striped sock was bad, the idea of how that poor woman had died was much, much worse. Simple exhaustion finally overcame my imagination, and I drifted off.

I came awake a few hours later, clawing the bedclothes and gulping at the air like a drowning woman. My throat ached. Where was that piercing shriek coming from?

Oh. That was me.

"What's wrong?!"

And that was Barr, struggling to a sitting position beside me and flipping on the bedside light.

"Sophie Mae! What's wrong?"

I let out a shaky breath and immediately sucked in another. My lips tingled, and I could feel my hands beginning to cramp. Great. I was hyperventilating. I squeezed my eyes shut and carefully slowed my breathing. "Sorry. Bad dream." A vague memory surfaced of crushing darkness, of nothingness—no light, no air. No hope.

No life.

"God, babe. C'mere." My sweetie wrapped his arms around me, and we sank back to the pillows.

Footsteps pounded on the stairs, and moments later a frantic-looking Meghan stood in the bedroom doorway, a sleepy Erin wandering up behind her. "What's the matter?"

So much for the door at the end of the hall. I sat up again.

"Just a bad dream," I said. "I'm sorry I woke you."

Relief flooded her face. "You sure?" She looked at Barr for confirmation.

He nodded. "Go back to bed."

"Are you okay, Sophie Mae?" Erin asked in a small voice.

"I'm fine, Bug. See you in the morning."

Meghan shepherded her daughter back downstairs.

I was still trembling. Barr flipped off the light.

"You want to talk about it?" he asked in a voice ripe with sleep.

"Nah. Thanks. You go on back to sleep."

Safely ensconced in his embrace, I stared at the window. A whisper of breeze made the curtain flutter. His soft snoring began in my ear. A hint of jasmine from the vine in the backyard curled into the room. The gray square of night outside offset the darkness of the rest of the bedroom but already beckoned with the surety of morning for yours truly.

The compost lady wasn't so lucky.

A kiss on my cheek woke me to full daylight Tuesday morning.

"I'm on my way," Barr murmured. "I'll call you later, okay?"

Rubbing my eyes with one hand, I raised up on the other elbow. "What time is it?"

"A little after seven, but I've got paperwork to do before the interview."

"Oh, God. I shouldn't have slept so long." I sat up and threw off the covers. "Another interview?" The department had been working through the applicants for the open detective position for weeks now. So far most of the candidates had been wildly inappropriate. Only one had piqued any interest, and she'd taken a job in Seattle.

"This one doesn't sound too great, either." He turned toward the door. "Some funny discrepancies in his work history Zahn needs to check out."

"Barr? Did you mean it about my helping you with this case?"

He turned back. "What did you have in mind?"

"I don't know. But I really want to do something. That poor woman died so horribly. Maybe I could show that picture around to the list Allie Turner gave you?" I'd come up with the idea before finally drifting off again right before dawn. "This afternoon all the members will be coming to the farm to pick up their vegetables and eggs for the week."

A slow nod from my husband. "Yeah." He looked thoughtful. "We need to find out who the Jane Doe is ASAP, and that would certainly save me some time."

I swung my feet to the floor. "Perfect. I'll lie in wait for them in the distribution shed."

He smiled and bent to kiss me again. "Do what you can, and I'll tell Zahn so he won't get his shorts in a twist when he finds out."

"Yessir." I felt better now that I had the go-ahead.

That dream had been a doozy. Even as I slipped into yoga pants and a T-shirt, it lingered like a bad odor on the edges of my thoughts.

Walking into the kitchen, I offered Meghan a hearty, if somewhat forced, "Good morning!"

"Good—" she looked up. "Oh, no."

I froze with my hand halfway to the coffeepot. "What?"

"You changed your mind."

"About . . . ?"

"I can tell. You're going to stick your nose into that woman's death." Her sigh was long and loud.

How did she do that? "How do you do that?" I poured my coffee.

"A bad dream that brought you awake screaming. Dark circles under your eyes—you hardly slept last night, thinking about her. But you're cheerful this morning anyway, complete with a bounce in your step. A bounce of purpose." Her jaw set. "I can *tell*."

My laugh ended with a little quiver. "Maybe you should be the one finding out who she is."

She held up her hand. "No thanks. I had quite enough yesterday." Her arm dropped. "Wait a second. The police still don't know who she is?"

"Nope." I took a sip. "But it was murder. No question." I paused for a beat. "And get this—she was buried alive."

Meghan's eyes widened. "No."

"Yes. Well, probably."

"That's . . . that's . . ."

I turned and looked at her over the steam curling out of my cup. "There aren't really any good words, are there?"

Eyes still showing a lot of white, she shook her head.

"I'm only going to try to find out who she was. Barr got a picture of her after they cleaned her all up and showed it to the Turners, but they didn't recognize her."

"He didn't show it to me," Meghan said. "He sat right there and ate blueberry pancakes this morning and never said a word."

"Pancakes—that's what I smell! Was Erin around? I bet that's why he didn't say anything."

She still didn't look happy.

"Wait here."

I ran upstairs and retrieved the picture from the bedroom. Glancing out the window, I saw Erin in the chicken pen. She'd been spending a lot of time with the hens lately, and she'd mentioned showing them at the upcoming Evergreen State Fair. Back in the kitchen, I shoved the photo at my friend.

With thumb and forefinger she took it from me. After a few moments loaded with hesitation, she flipped it over. A quick glance, and she looked away. "Nope. Sorry."

I took it from her, peering at that pretty face. Ruth was right. She didn't look very old. Mid-twenties was my guess. "Are you sure? You didn't look at it very long."

Meghan sighed and held out her hand. This time she stared at it for a long time. Finally she licked her lips and looked up at me. "I feel like I should know her."

My pulse quickened. "Well, do you or don't you?"

One side of her mouth quirked up in apology. "Maybe I just wish I did."

Well, heck. So did I. My shoulders slumped.

My housemate sat down at the table. "I'm sorry."

"Don't be silly. I'm sure someone will recognize her." I changed the subject. "Are there any pancakes left?"

"Barr grabbed the last two when he left. I could make more, though."

"Nah, that's okay." I slid into a chair and leaned my elbows on the butcher block table. "I bet there are still plenty of blueberries, though."

She laughed and got up, opening the refrigerator. "Tons. I was going to freeze some this afternoon." We'd been eating up all the fresh berries we got from the farm share, so the previous weekend Meghan, Erin, and I had trooped out to a U-pick farm to load up on freezables.

I pulled the photo toward me again, grimacing at the woman's closed eyelids. "I wonder what color her eyes were."

Meghan put a bowl of fresh blueberries dripping in cream on the table by my elbow and leaned over my shoulder. "Hard to tell. Who knows whether that was even her natural hair color."

"No one dyes their hair such a dull color, do they?"

"That looks like the bird lady," Erin said from my other side.

"Erin!" Meghan straightened up so fast I thought she'd throw out her back.

I whisked the photo under the table. "You sneaked up on us."

"It's not my fault if you're too busy to hear me come in. What's with the picture?"

I cocked my head. "Did you mean the bird lady in your novel?" Actually, her book sounded more fantastical than fantasy, given the increasingly crazy stuff Erin talked about now and again. For example, one character was an old lady who was part flamingo—pink hair, had a habit of standing on one leg, inordinately fond of fish. Erin called her the bird lady.

Now she looked at me with pity. "Of course not. My bird lady isn't a real person, Sophie Mae."

I took her note of condescension as my due. "Then what did you mean?"

She went to the counter and extracted an oatmeal cookie from the jar. "I dunno."

"Do, too," I said.

"Erin! You just had breakfast!" Meghan chided.

"So? This is my breakfast dessert," her daughter said and disappeared down the hall to her bedroom.

That little stinker knew something.

Meghan turned to me in wonder. "She is just out and out defying me."

"Um, yeah. Didn't you do that as a kid?"

"Of course not."

I blinked. "Really?"

"I got along great with my parents."

"That's not the point. You and Erin get along great, too. Now she's testing your boundaries."

"Well, I don't like it." Worry creased my friend's forehead.

I got up to give her a hug. "This isn't like you. You've always handled your rather amazing kid with such grace and ease. You can't fold when things start to get difficult."

"I know that. I just don't know how to handle her."

"The same way you always have. With love and reason."

"I guess."

"She's the same kid, only she's starting that journey to being a grown-up. One day she'll be a real, live, functional adult in society."

She shook her head. "Yeah, yeah. I get that. I don't know what's wrong with me. Maybe I'm starting menopause."

I barked a laugh. "At thirty-eight? You'd better not be!"

"Are you sick, Mom?" Erin asked from the kitchen doorway.

Now Meghan laughed. "No."

"Okay. Good." Erin held out a book. "This is what that lady in the picture reminded me of."

I put the photo I'd been holding face down on the counter and took the slim volume. It was a book on birds of prey, open to a section about merlins. My eyebrows knitted as I skimmed the text and noted the depiction of a small, hook-beaked face with dark eyes looking out at me.

"I don't get it."

Erin said, "She told me all about those little birds. Is that who you found, Mom? Is that a picture of a dead person?"

Meghan frowned and picked up the photo again. Her eyes roved over it, drinking in details she couldn't bear to look at ten minutes earlier. Erin edged closer, but Meghan automatically held it so her daughter wouldn't get another look at the "dead person."

"Geesh, you don't have to be so weird about it. With Sophie Mae around, one of these days *I'll* be the one to find a body."

I pulled her to my side and put my hand over her grinning mouth. "Hush, you little imp."

She shook her head. "Mmmph."

"Bug, where do you remember her from?" Meghan asked.

I removed my hand from Erin's mouth but not my grip on her shoulder, and she said, "Didn't you give her massages? Afternoons after I got home from school?"

A new light sparked in Meghan's eyes. "Oh, my God. I think you might be right. That was what? Four years ago, at least. Maybe five. And she only came to me a couple times."

I could barely contain my glee. I might have a clue for Barr after all!

My housemate went on. "She didn't look like this, though. Her hair was longer, and lighter. She used to be heavier, too."

"But who *is* she?" Doing my best to tamp down my impatience.

"Well, if Erin's right, she was some kind of ornithologist. I sure don't remember." She put the picture back on the counter and came over to us. Ruffling her daughter's hair, she said, "How on earth did you remember her from that one glimpse you had of the picture?"

Erin shrugged under my palms. "She talked to me about those birds. The little hunters."

I squeezed her shoulders. "You've been a big help, Bug. Really big."

"Okay. Good." She twisted in my grasp. "Will you let go of me now? I need to meet Zoe so we can work on her 4-H project, and I'm late."

I released my grip, and she was out the door. I turned back to her mother. "So she was an ornithologist—a bird lady—who liked to get massages. But what's her *name*?"

The smile dropped from Meghan's face. She looked at me helplessly. "I don't have the vaguest clue."

EIGHT

I CALLED BARR WHILE Meghan went into her office to go through her files hoping to recognize a name that would go with the picture. He didn't answer—probably in the middle of interviewing that potential detective—so I left the information about the ornithology connection on his voicemail. "Sorry, no name yet, though. I'm still planning to go out to the farm and talk to the members. Call me when you get a chance."

Frustrated, I cleaned up the kitchen and did the breakfast dishes. How could I find out who the bird lady was? Search online for "Washington State ornithologist"? Well, it couldn't hurt.

"Hey, Sophie Mae! How's it going?"

I turned to find Cyan Waters standing in the doorway at the top of the stairs that led down to the basement. Several months previously I'd given her a key to the back door, which greatly simplified the way we coordinated our schedules. She wore blue shorts and a T-shirt that said Smile—It's Free. Kalie hovered on the step behind her.

"Hey, yourself. Is it eight already?" I shot a glance at the clock. Sure enough, straight up eight.

"Yep. Whatcha got for us today?"

"Lip balms and foot scrub. Hi, Kalie."

The thin, quiet brunette behind Cyan sketched a shy wave. "Hi."

"How many?" Cyan asked, bouncing on the balls of her feet.

"Half a gross of lemon lip balms and half a gross of cinnamon. Sixty jars of peppermint foot scrub. And do me a favor? Put the *pickup* sign out front so UPS Joe knows to stop. I put all the outgoing boxes by the back door. Oh, and here's his usual bribe." I dropped three oatmeal cookies in a bag and held it out to her. UPS Joe liked sweet treats, and I liked not having to haul boxes out to the front of the house.

"Okey dokey." She grabbed the bag with a grin and turned to go back downstairs. Kalie had already disappeared from view.

"I'll be down in a sec to get you started."

She turned back. "That's okay. I mean, unless you've got something else you're working on, we can take care of the lip balms and scrub. No problem."

I hesitated, doing battle with my inner control freak. She didn't really need supervision for everyday production. Heck, once she'd run Winding Road for a whole week by herself.

"Thanks, Cyan. And I love your hair. When did you do that?"

She grinned. "Yesterday. Thanks!"

"That was the color of my wedding gown, you know."

"No kidding? Cool!" And with a toss of her aubergine locks she clattered down the stairs.

She was my right-hand woman when it came to Winding Road. Efficient, effective, and a hard worker, she could do pretty much everything except the books. And did. She'd even suggested I hire Kalie, who, though she was timid, worked hard and did a good job.

I finished mopping up after the pancakes I'd missed out on and went upstairs to take a shower.

"Any luck?" I asked my housemate.

My online search had netted me a big fat nothing. The Washington State Ornithological Society had photos but no member list. None of the birders looked like our dead woman. There was no guarantee she would have joined the society anyway, but at least it was an avenue Barr or Sergeant Zahn could follow up if I didn't have any luck determining the identity of the compost, er, bird lady.

Meghan looked up from where she hunched over her desk. "I skimmed my files from four and five years ago, hoping the name alone would spark a memory, but it didn't."

"Do you think Erin could be wrong?"

She shrugged. "I'd wonder if I didn't remember the woman at all. But that kid has practically got a photographic memory, and I do recall that face. Sort of. Now I'm going through each file one by one to see if I can remember any particular physical complaints."

"That's good," I said. "But let's put that on hold. I have another idea."

She sat back and waited.

"I want to show everyone two photos."

She raised her eyebrows in question.

"You said the bird lady looked a lot different four-five years ago, right?"

"Uh, huh."

"And you haven't run into her since then."

She grimaced.

"Alive, I mean."

"No. Not to the best of my knowledge."

"So maybe she lived in the area, left, and then came back. Maybe Jake or Bette knew her then, too. Maybe even Ruth. However, like you, they didn't recognize her because she looks different. What we need is another photo that shows what she looked like then."

She nodded. "Okay. But where do you propose getting the new photo?"

"From Bette Anders." Our friend Bette, the potter, made a decent living with her clay artistry, having built a good name and loyal clientele. "She was at the farm when you found the body, and Barr showed her the autopsy photo last night. So we wouldn't inadvertently compromise the investigation if we asked for her help," I said.

Meghan had changed into a coral-toned calico dress that set off her eyes, and now she leaned back in her chair and smoothed the skirt. "I still don't get it."

"You know those clay masks she sculpts? She told me she uses facial manipulation software to work out ideas, since the masks are based on photos of real people. See, I want to scan this picture—" I waved the one in my hand. "—so we have a digital copy. Then take it to Bette and have her use her whippy software to change the face to reflect the way your bird lady looked four years ago."

She looked skeptical. "That sounds like a lot of trouble."

"Meghan, I really, really want to find out who she was. I'm willing to try anything."

Her head tipped to one side. "All right. Go for it. I don't have a client for a few hours, so I'll continue to plod through these." She waved at the stack of folders on one side of her desk. "That way we'll be coming at the problem from two fronts."

For someone who was dead set against my getting involved, my housemate was pretty willing to get involved her own self. Interesting.

"I like your thinking except for one problem," I said.

"What?"

"I don't know what she used to look like. You do. You have to come with me to give Bette some direction."

"Hmm." The idea didn't please her, but then she seemed to make a decision. "Well, I don't even know what I'm looking for here. Nothing seems to be jogging my memory." She closed the file that was open on her desk. "When do you want to go?"

"She's an early riser. I bet she's hard at work now. I'll give her a call."

"Are you sure you should interrupt her?"

"I wouldn't bother her if it weren't for a good cause," I said. "And I saw her face at the farm yesterday. She was horrified. I bet she'll be happy to help."

At least I hoped so.

The phone rang five times before Bette picked up. I apologized for calling so early.

"No problem," she said. "You know me. I've been up for hours."

"Well, I'm about to interrupt your morning even more, if you'll let me."

"Egg delivery?" Bette was one of Erin's regular customers.

"No. I mean, sure, I can bring over a dozen if you want them, but I'm in need of a favor. You know that software you told me about a while back? Where you can manipulate facial features?"

"... yeah."

"I was hoping you might perform some of your magic on a photo for me."

"Um, sure. When were you thinking—"

"How about right now? Meghan and I can be there in five minutes."

"Uh, okay ..."

"Great! See you in a few."

She was saying goodbye as I hung up. Dang it, Kelly was right. This investigating stuff was kind of exciting. I didn't dare hope this little scheme would work though.

Oh, poo, I thought as I went downstairs. I did too hope it would work. After quickly checking in on the girls—who had already finished pouring the lemon lip balms and had moved on to melting beeswax for the cinnamon ones—I scanned the picture into the computer in my workroom. Then I copied it to a flash drive, shut off the monitor, and went back up to the kitchen.

"Meghan!" I slipped the drive into my pocket. "Are you ready?"

Bette lived alone in the middle of the next block on our street. Well, alone except for Alexander, her German shepherd. He sat on the front porch, regal and still as a stone as we entered through the gate and closed it behind us. It wasn't until we reached the bottom step that his jaws stretched in a wide yawn, ending in a toothy grin. Rising, his brushy tail swept back and forth a few times before he trotted down to greet Brodie. Old friends, they nosed each other. Then Alexander ducked down on his forepaws, his behind in the air, an invitation to play. Brodie let out a yip and ran at him, ready to give it a go despite his creaky old joints.

Moments later Bette appeared on the other side of the screen door, wiping her hands on a rag. "Hey, you two. Come on in."

We left Brodie in the fenced yard with Alexander. Inside, I held out the dozen eggs I'd remembered to grab from the fridge at the last minute. She took them with a smile. "Thanks! Let me get my wallet." Her deep voice resonated in the tiny entryway.

I waved her offer of money away. "Consider it a favor for a favor. I'll settle up with Erin."

"Hard to argue with that."

We followed her down the short hallway to what in most homes would have been the living room. Bette wasn't most people, though, and had transformed the big square space into a studio. She'd expanded the windows in the two exterior walls to let in as much natural light as possible. Another wall was floor to ceiling shelves crowded with masks and pots and free-form sculptures in various stages of creation. Four tables in the main room each held a different project, an electric potter's wheel sat in one corner, and large, plastic-wrapped blocks of clay and buckets of the slimy mixture of clay and water called slip marched down another wall.

The space around the windows was covered with finished masks. Most were caricatures, some funny and some edging on harsh. A few were quite realistic, though, almost looking like they'd respond if you spoke to them. The place vibrated with her talent and creativity.

The doorway to the kitchen had been enlarged so the two rooms flowed into each other, and I could see the kitchen table piled with bottles and jars, along with sponges and brushes for applying paints and glazes. Bette had installed an industrial sink at one end, opposite the regular sink she presumably used for such mundane tasks as washing vegetables and dishes.

Despite the brightly lit rooms, every time I entered Bette's house I had the impression I'd somehow gone underground. It smelled like I imagined the center of the earth would, like clay and dirt with a metallic undertone of the minerals in so many of the glazes she used. This morning the aromas of toast and coffee also rode the air, fitting oddly into the rest of the atmosphere. A basket of multi-colored tomatoes from the last CSA share hunkered near the stove.

In the several years I'd known her—ever since moving in with Meghan and Erin—I'd never seen Bette wear any makeup or any clothing that wasn't smudged with a bit of clay spatter. Most of the time "smudge" didn't even begin to cover it. Today she wore faded denim jeans cinched at the waist with an oversized leather belt and a yellow tank top, all liberally smeared with white clay and splotches of something darker.

The chaos she managed to live with would have driven me crazy, but it seemed to fuel her creativity, so who was I to care? We weren't best friends, but she was nice as could be and made a mean batch of bread-and-butter pickles to boot. Over the years we'd socialized on a semi-regular basis, but since we'd both joined the CSA I saw her more often. We'd had several conversations about the best way to grow various flowers and vegetables. Her backyard dahlia garden alone could have supplied enough blooms for two florists.

"Now, what's this about a picture?" she asked, leading us into the kitchen and opening the refrigerator. She put the eggs on the top shelf and turned back to us.

A whippy Mac laptop connected to a 21-inch monitor sat on an old trestle table in the corner. I liked the juxtaposition of the ultra-modern technology perched on a piece of furniture that looked to be over a hundred years old. I took out the flash drive and gave it to her. She sat down in a battered ladder-back chair and plugged it in.

"I should warn you," I said. "You've seen this picture before."

She looked the question at me. I could see a whisper of understanding enter her eyes before I answered.

"Yep. It's the woman Barr showed you last night. From the farm."

NINE

Bette frowned and looked at Meghan, who lifted her palms to the ceiling. "We're trying to find out who she is. I think I've met her, but she looked different then. Sophie Mae thinks if we make the photo look more like what I remember, someone else may be able to tell us her name."

"Oh." The one word held a surprising amount of resistance. "I don't know if I like the idea of getting mixed up with that."

Meghan and I exchanged glances. So much for being happy to help. But in the back of my mind I'd known this reaction was possible. It was why I hadn't told Bette the whole story on the phone. Not everyone was gung ho about crime solving. I dragged another chair over. Straddling it backwards, I settled my jean-clad behind on the seat and leaned forward until she looked me in the eye.

Trying to channel Brodie's best begging look, the one he used almost exclusively for bacon, I said, "Please? Barr probably has access to the same kind of software at the state crime lab. But that would take a lot more time—and time is of the essence in a murder investigation." At least that's what they said on TV.

Her expression didn't alter a whit.

"See, the police department is kind of short handed right now, so we're trying to help out."

Nothing.

"Bette, we're already right here," Meghan prompted. "Can't you at least try?"

Our friend looked up at her and licked her lips. Then she let out a whoosh of air. "Yeah, I guess."

So much for my Brodie look. "Thank you," I said.

Bette hunched over the laptop, manipulating the touchpad. The screen sprang to life, and she clicked on an icon on the desktop. A face filled the screen, apparently the last file she had been working on. It was the photo of a young man. She had adjusted the planes of his face, exaggerating some elements and downplaying others to create a face that was his and not his at the same time. No wonder her masks were so popular.

In fact, Barr's birthday was coming up in another month or so. I'd been wracking my brain trying to find the perfect gift, and here the idea was being handed to me on a plate. Nice.

A few moments later she had loaded my scanned photo, and the bird lady's face replaced the young man's.

"God," Bette whispered. She cleared her throat, looking a little green. "What do you want to change?"

Meghan dragged another chair over to sit on Bette's other side. She looked a little green around the gills, too. "Can you add a little weight to her face?"

She pointed the cursor, clicked and dragged.

"I was thinking more along her jaw line," my housemate said. "The bone structure should stay the same."

More clicking and dragging.

Beside me, Meghan shook her head. "No, that's not quite right either."

"Well, I'm doing the best I can," Bette said. "I'm used to making people look less real, not more."

"I know, and we appreciate you doing this." I looked at Meghan.

"I'm sorry, Bette," she said. "I don't even have a clear idea of what I want to change."

"Didn't you say the hair was longer?" I asked.

Meghan nodded. "Can we add about four inches, and maybe some curl? And make it a few shades lighter?"

Bette did as she was asked. Back and forth they went, my patient housemate providing suggestions while Bette tried to follow them. Finally, Meghan stood up with a relieved expression. "I think that's as close as we can get."

The bird lady did look significantly different. "Is there any way you could make her look a little … more lively?" I'd almost said, "Less dead?"

Bette made a sound of distaste.

"You mean like a smile or something?" Meghan asked me, her own lip curling in disgust.

"Uh, no," I said with a pointed look. "That would be creepy. But could you brighten the color? That blue tinge makes her look like … well, like a vampire."

Bette moused over some controls, clicking away, and a lighter, yellow tone replaced the blue wash. It didn't really look better, but at least the woman didn't appear as if she was about to turn into a bat.

"That's great." I stood and moved around to face Bette. "Barr said he showed you the first picture last night. How about this one? Does she look familiar now?"

She looked up at me, then back at her screen. Her lips thinned into a horizontal line. "No."

My shoulders slumped. "Oh, well. Maybe it'll jostle someone else's memory. I'm going to take both versions out to the Turners' and ask around during the vegetable distribution this afternoon. Can you save a copy to my flash drive?"

She peered at the screen again, drinking in the image.

"Bette?" I prompted.

"Sure." She saved the picture, closed the program, and stood. Handing me the drive, she said, "Well, good luck. I guess I'll see you out at the farm later." She seemed more relaxed now that she wasn't staring at the picture of a murder victim. I couldn't really blame her.

Bette had never struck me as the hugging type, so I held out my hand and we shook. "Thanks again. I know it was a pain, but maybe something will pan out. I know Barr will be grateful for your help, too."

She nodded. "I hope you find out what happened to her."

"Me, too." I walked through to the living room/studio. Behind me, Meghan walked up to Bette and gave her a big squeeze, which our much taller friend returned with enthusiasm. Huh. So much for my read on her. Of course, Meghan had that effect on people.

Outside, Alexander and Brodie had collapsed panting onto the grass, their faces turned up to the sun. When we came out to the porch both got up, and our corgi grinned and waddled over to Meghan. She bent down and smoothed the fur between his ears while I ruffled the thick, dark fluff around the German shepherd's neck. On the public sidewalk out front, we latched the gate and waved goodbye to Bette standing in the doorway before setting off briskly for home.

"Is it always so hard to get people to help when you do your little investigations?" Meghan asked.

Ignoring her reference to my *little* investigations, I said, "Not always, but sometimes. A lot of people would rather stick their heads in the sand than get involved."

She was silent for several steps. "Like me, you mean."

"Nah. I didn't mean you in particular. But I bet you understand why some folks are resistant. They'd rather live their safe little lives and not think about the fact that bad stuff does happen, and often right next door. Or even closer."

Her chin dipped in thought. "Yeah. I get it. Now I'm starting to see why you tend to jump in with both feet."

I began to protest, but she held up her hand. "You do it because it matters. Because someone has to, especially since so many other people don't. I bet that's how Barr feels about his job, too."

I stopped in front of our house, breathing in the scent of the tea rose that twined up one corner of the porch support. "I hadn't really tried to pick it apart like that, but yeah—you're right." I turned and met her gaze. "It matters."

The front door was unlocked.

"Erin? You home?" Meghan called, propping it open all the way to let the warming breeze inside.

No answer. We looked at each other.

"I thought you locked up when we left," I said.

"I did."

Music started up in Erin's room then. Meghan rolled her eyes and headed down the hallway. I headed toward the kitchen and the stairs to the basement. I wanted to see how the girls were getting on with Winding Road business and print out copies of the bird lady's picture.

"Erin?" I heard Meghan say, and paused. "Can I come in?"

Poking my head around the corner, I saw my friend standing in front of Erin's closed door. Hmm. Two days in a row. That couldn't be good.

I didn't hear the response, but Meghan said, "Well, I'm coming in anyway." She twisted the knob, then stood in the open doorway, her mouth agape. "*What* do you think you're doing?"

Uh, oh. I padded down the hallway to join them.

Erin sat on the bed, feet dangling above the floor, glaring at her mother. At least I thought she was glaring—it was kind of hard to tell with the peacock blues and greens around her eyes. Also, she was blinking a million miles a minute, and tears streamed from her reddened right eye. The telltale smear of black underneath betrayed her attempts to apply mascara.

"Ow," I said. "Stuck yourself in the eye with the applicator, huh."

Beside me Meghan was quiet. Really quiet. Scary quiet.

Erin said, "Can you show me how to do it right?"

I glanced at her mother. "Um. Maybe later, okay? Right now we should wash out your eye."

She waved her hand at me. "Oh, it's all right. I cried the goo right out. It doesn't even hurt now."

Meghan opened her mouth. Closed it again without saying anything. That meant she didn't trust herself to speak.

I took a step forward. "I don't really think green is your best color, Erin. Or blue."

She bristled.

"See, you want eye shadow to show off your eyes, not dominate them. A nice, soft mushroomy color, maybe with a little smudge of pink, would emphasize the pretty gray in yours."

Erin knew her mother was on the edge of blowing, and she dealt with it by carefully ignoring her. Now she slid off the bed and went to her desk, where she'd propped a mirror against her computer. She gazed into it, turning this way and that.

"Huh. I guess I see what you mean." She faced us. "Seems like a lot of trouble, though. I don't know how anyone can get that gunk to stay on their eyelashes anyway."

"Go wash your face," Meghan said.

Erin scooted past her and went down the hallway.

I laughed. "Do you think it's because she loves Halloween so much?"

Meghan gave me a look that would have withered every single plant in the Turners' greenhouse.

I grinned back at her. "Let's make lunch. I'm starving."

In the kitchen we stuffed soft goat cheese, slow-roasted tomatoes, and fresh lettuce into chewy pita shells. Then we drizzled homemade yogurt mixed with grated cucumber and ground cumin over the top to create a kind of vegetarian gyro. Meghan went to get Erin out of the bathroom, and I went down to see if Cyan and Kalie were interested in joining us.

They were, so I sent them upstairs and ducked into the storeroom. Plugging the flash drive into the computer, I set a half-dozen copies printing before returning to the kitchen.

Erin had managed to remove the first layer of colors, but there were still hints of blue and green, and her right eye was still pretty pink. But she tucked into her pita sandwich with enthusiasm. Gradually her mother's ire lifted.

Good thing, because I was getting tired of playing referee.

TEN

After lunch one of Meghan's regular clients showed up. I didn't know his name, but he was a big, hairy guy I'd seen several times before. I spent a few hours helping Cyan and Kalie finish up the foot scrub, then set them to packing more orders into boxes while I inventoried my supplies and made lists of items to order. At a bit before three o'clock we were finished with the Winding Road tasks for the day and began planning the next day's work. It felt like a luxury, not having to put in twelve hours before feeling like I was finally on top of things.

It also worked out well because CSA members would be stopping by to pick up their shares at Turner Farm starting at four o'clock and continue to straggle in until seven. I planned to get there early and stay late.

"Do you want to come with me?" I asked Meghan. Big hairy guy had left, and she was wiping flour off the counter. Two loaves of bread rose under a clean dish towel on the table. "It'll be the perfect opportunity to see everyone."

She shook her head. "I'll leave that to you."

"Sure?"

"I've still got one more client coming in, and then a pile of blueberries to freeze."

Guilt arrowed through me. "You've been doing more than your fair share lately. Wait to prep the berries, and I'll help tonight. Or tomorrow." Or when I could get to it.

But she waved away my protestation. "The workload around here always works out in the end. Besides, I've had enough of looking at that poor woman's photo for a while and don't envy you having to show it around even more."

"I'll go with you," Erin piped up.

"No, you won't," her mother said. "I'll need some help making dinner."

"Mo ... ommm," was the whining response.

"If you're old enough to wear eye shadow, you're old enough to mix up the rub for the baby-back ribs. Get out the kosher salt, chili powder, thyme, and brown sugar to start."

"Geesh," Erin grumbled as she went to the cupboard and began pulling out spices. "I'm not even going to wear eye shadow any more. Cyan told me my eyes are prettier without any distraction."

Now why hadn't I thought of that? I grinned at Meghan.

She made a face back. "Grab a few extra summer squash, okay? I want to make up a bunch of zucchini bread to freeze."

"Sure." I slung my tote bag over my shoulder and headed for the door. "See you later."

The bumper of Tom Turner's stepside Chevy was snugged up to the side of the farm stand. As I pulled my old Land Rover in beside it, he nodded to me and hefted a crate of glossy purple eggplants to his shoulder. Another crate of multi-colored peppers sat in the bed of the truck.

The shutters on the front of the small stand were open, and tilted wooden bins displayed the surplus vegetables available to the public. The Turners didn't have time or manpower to have someone waiting on the infrequent customers, so they relied on the honor system for the few hours per day it was open to the public. People took what they wanted and left their payment in the wide-mouthed Mason jar. So far that had worked out well, a gratifying testament to the good nature of most folks.

He carried the eggplants inside as I grabbed the file folder with the photos and opened my driver's door.

"Hey, Tom."

He placed the last one in a bin. "Hey, Sophie Mae. You're here early."

"And I'll be sticking around for a while. We have an updated picture of the woman Meghan found yesterday, and I want to show it—and the original—to the farm members, see if anyone recognizes her."

He frowned. "Let me see." He held out his hand.

I gave him the picture, and watched his face carefully. Was that a flicker of recognition? Or was I just making that up?

"Do you know her?" I pushed.

"She looks different here." He looked up at me. "Different than the photo your husband showed us last night, I mean."

"That's the idea."

His eyes searched my face, but I didn't offer more of an explanation. He returned both renditions of the bird lady. "Sorry. I can't help you." Abrupt.

Or wouldn't help me. Curiouser and curiouser. Barr definitely needed to follow up with Mr. Turner. "Is your wife around?"

"She's at the house." His words were clipped.

"How about Hallie and Nate?"

He shrugged. "Hallie took Clarissa shopping at that mall in Lynnwood. God knows what they'll come home with this time. Nate's around here someplace. I'll tell him you're looking for him."

"Thanks. Anything you need me to do while I'm hanging out?"

Tom considered. "Well, the popcorn needs to be picked sooner than later, so it can dry out of the weather. You could get started on that. Take the yard cart out to the field, and we'll store the ears in the back of the farm stand here."

Oh, wow. Homegrown popcorn. An image arose of sitting in the living room with Barr and Erin, Meghan and Kelly, eating from a huge bowl of warm, fluffy kernels loaded with butter and sprinkled with salt. Throw in the wind howling outside, an applewood fire crackling on the hearth, and a big jigsaw puzzle, and it sounded pretty much like my idea of heaven.

"Sounds good!" I grabbed a couple of canvas shopping bags from the back of the Rover and walked around to the distribution shed.

Volunteers took turns harvesting the farm produce on Tuesday mornings before pickup and then arranging it so members could drop by and help themselves. The double, barn-style doors at the end of the small building were wide open to let in light and air. The dusty pile of burlap bags I'd perched on to take my temperature the day before—was it really only yesterday?—now bulged with freshly picked goodies. They sat on the floor and lay open on the rustic tables that ran around the perimeter. Two scales nestled between the bags so people could measure out the vegetables offered by weight. A dry erase board on the back wall listed what was available for each member's share that week.

9 tomatoes
3 bell peppers
1 acorn squash
6 ears corn
½ pound raspberries
1 pound green or wax beans
1 cucumber
1 eggplant
1 head lettuce
1 oz. parsley
2 oz. basil
As much kale and zucchini as you can stand

We hadn't eaten much kale before participating in the CSA, so it had been a challenge to know what to do with all of it. Kale, it turned out, grew really well in the Pacific Northwest, and there was always some left over after everyone had picked up their share. So far we'd tried it in soup and stir-fries, cooked it in peanut sauce with Thai basil for a tasty side dish, and even added it to hummus. But my favorite way to eat kale so far was kale chips. Dressed with a little oil and kosher salt and then baked all crispy in the oven, they were pretty darn awesome. Not homemade potato chip awesome, mind you, but close.

As for the zucchini, everyone in the house was already a fan, even Barr. We never seemed to get as many as we wanted from the one start we planted each year in our small backyard garden. That might sound crazy, but cool, damp northwest summers don't always make for the best summer squash. So we were glad to take some overages. Besides Meghan's zucchini bread, it was necessary for good ratatouille and minestrone soup, great added to frittatas and fritters, grilled in big rounds and doused with mustard, or sliced thin and sautéed in brown butter with basil. My dad had even passed on his recipe for zucchini Carpaccio.

Each week there seemed to be a glut of something new at the farm. Lately, the pole beans had been going crazy. As long as I was going to be hanging around, I would try to trade the lettuce and parsley from our share for more green beans, and see if there were any left at the end. We had plenty of salad makings in our backyard garden, but extra beans could be pickled or frozen. All part of the plan to stock up for the winter. Soon we'd be getting root vegetables like beets, carrots, parsnips, and turnips in the share, and we already had a plan for a makeshift root cellar—bins of sand in a cool crawl space—to keep them fresh for months.

I loaded up the bags, leaving the items I hoped to trade in the distribution shed, grabbed some extra zucchini for Meghan's bread and some extra kale to make more of those strangely yummy chips, and hauled everything out to the Rover. As I shut my door, Tom climbed into his truck and started the engine.

I went over and leaned into the window opening. “Barr mentioned Nate was gone last night.”

He nodded. “Went to a movie.”

“Who was his date?”

One shoulder lifted and dropped. “Guess you’d have to ask him.”

I smiled ruefully. My guess was Daphne Sparks. I’d seen how they clung to each other in the wake of the bird lady’s discovery.

A car I didn’t recognize pulled into the parking lot. A young girl gazed at me through the window as a stout woman got out. “I’ll be right back,” the woman said to her, grabbing a basket from the back seat and striding toward the distribution shed. I waved goodbye to Tom and trailed along after her.

“Excuse me,” I said from the doorway.

Her eyes flicked to the list on the dry erase board, and she reached for a dimple-skinned cucumber. “Yes?” She grabbed the eggplant next, sparing me an impatient glance.

I held out the photos. “Do you recognize this woman?”

Her gaze raked across them before returning to the share list. “Never seen her. Why?”

“We’re just trying to identify her.”

She stopped and turned, finally curious. “Why? Who is she?”

“No one seems to know. She was found … nearby. Deceased. She might have had some kind of connection to the farm.”

“She’s dead? Good Lord! Let me see that again.”

I handed her the pictures.

“Where did they find her? Is this her sister? Were there two of them? Are you with the police? How did she die? How come I didn't hear about this on the news?" The questions came fast, and her voice got louder with each one until she sounded smack dab on the edge of hysteria.

I chose to answer the last one and duck the rest. "No doubt it will be in the *Cadyville Eye* tomorrow. Are you sure you don't know who she is?"

She shook her head with real regret. "Gosh. No. Sorry."

As she left, Allie passed her in the doorway. Her face was pinched with distress, but she seemed a little less vague than when I'd left yesterday. The shock of a dead body in the compost had worn off, but now an aura of deep anxiety surrounded her.

"Tom said you have another picture to show me," she said.

"I do." I held it out. "How are you doing with all this?"

Allie grimaced. "Awful. I'm glad Hallie took Clarissa out. I don't think I'm very good at hiding how worried I am."

"It'll all work out," I said.

She looked me straight in the eye. "Thanks for your kindness. Really. But you can't know that. You just can't. We put everything we have into this farm. If it goes under, we won't have anything left." Tears threatened, but she swallowed and clenched her jaw. "Doesn't do any good to think like that, though. I have to have faith."

"Faith is good," I said, feeling a little lame.

"It sure is. And a lot of that faith rests on your husband's ability to find out why that woman was killed, and who did it. Barr has to fix the reputation of Turner Farm."

That was a lot to ask. I didn't say that, though, only nodded. "First he has to know who she was."

Her hands were shaking as she looked at the updated bird lady. She stood in the light of the doorway and looked at it for a really long time before giving a single, abrupt shake of her head. "I don't know her. I wish I did, but I don't." Her voice was tight. "We haven't gotten to know that many people. We spend all our time keeping things going here."

"It's okay," I said, putting a hand on her shoulder. She covered it with her own hand and hung her head. We stood there for a long moment.

Finally, she swallowed audibly. "Okay. I have to get back to work. Thank you, Sophie Mae."

Allie trudged back toward the farmhouse, and I watched her go. Something was off here, but I couldn't put my finger on it. Maybe it was only the fear of losing everything they'd worked for.

Everything is a lot.

ELEVEN

I MADE MENTAL NOTES of what to tell Barr as I tracked down the yard cart as Tom had suggested and pulled it out to the nearby field of popcorn. Arnold Ziffel tried to follow, but I explained he wasn't allowed in the corn field and shut the gate in his face. Soon more cars arrived, so I returned to the distribution shed to quiz more members about the bird lady. It was fun to meet some new people and see old friends, but no one seemed to know who she was. Most really tried to be helpful, though a couple got kind of pale, and one roundly chastised me for showing the pictures at all. I would have felt better about the whole thing if the two different pictures didn't cause more confusion than anything else. I silently berated myself for wasting Meghan and Bette's time earlier in the day. Not to mention my own. All that silliness about me being good at finding things out must have gone to my head.

I didn't advertise that the body had been found about a hundred yards away at the bottom of the Turners' compost pile, but my discretion went out the window when Jake Beagle showed up with his booming voice and big personality.

Fortunately about half the members had already come and gone by that time, but he began regaling the few still loading up on vegetables with details from the day before. They'd already denied knowing who she was, and it didn't seem right to keep gossiping about the details of the body's unearthing. I also felt protective of the Turners and their farm—even more so after talking with Allie. The CSA might not be able to withstand a bad reputation just as it was getting off the ground. Never mind that the town newspaper would give plenty of details about where she'd been found. At least it only came out once a week.

"Um. Jake," I interrupted.

"What? You were here." He laughed. "Well, of course *you* were here!"

"Take a look." I shook the pictures in his face, hoping to distract him.

"What's this? Oh, this is what Felicia was talking about last night."

I remembered Barr had told me Jake's wife had seen the autopsy photo. "You weren't home, then?"

"My week at the Walk-In Clinic." He fished a pair of reading glasses out of his shirt pocket and peered at both versions of the bird lady. "Well, now."

My heartbeat quickened.

"Why are these so different?"

"Meghan remembered her from four or five years ago. So we made a few alterations to match her memory."

"Huh." Mr. Gossip seemed at a loss for words.

"Do you know her?" I prompted for the umpteenth time.

He snapped his fingers, and I jumped. "Patient. I bet she came to see me for some malady or other. Must have been a while ago, though. You know, I'm not so great with names, but I never forget a face."

I tried to hide the irritation that always surfaced when I heard someone brag about that. Faces without names weren't much good in the best of circumstances.

Jake left soon after, and I found myself alone in the dusty shed. I straightened the scales, tidied the piles of vegetables, and folded a few empty bags. In between showing the photos, I'd haggled for more green beans, so I took them out to the Rover. The sky had grown overcast, cooling the late summer afternoon significantly. A vee formation of Canada geese honked their way south overhead, and I paused to breathe in the scent of growing things.

A little after six o'clock, I emptied the second load of popcorn into the small storeroom behind the farm stand. Straightening, I saw a plume of dust on the road and then the sporty red Camaro that caused it. It pulled into the driveway of the Turners' house at the edge of the farthest field. Hallie and Clarissa removed a shopping bag from the trunk and took it inside.

I debated whether to go talk to Allie's sister and track down Nate while I was at it. Only a half dozen people still had to pick up their shares, and I sure hadn't had much luck so far. My phone rang, and I hauled it out of my pocket.

It was Barr. "How's it going?"

"Crappy. Dull. Lonely. You got my message about your victim being interested in birds?" I asked.

"Yeah, thanks. That's progress at least, and now I've got someone going through missing person reports looking for a female ornithologist in her mid-to-late twenties. Lonely? Isn't there anyone else there at the farm?"

"I saw Hallie pull up to the house, and Tom and Allie are here. Nate, too, though I haven't seen him yet."

"When I agreed to your plan I thought there'd be lots of people around. I don't like you being there by yourself."

"I hear something outside." I craned my head and looked out the door. "It's Bette, on her bike. Feel better?"

"Hmm."

"Listen, I left you a copy of the picture she updated—or backdated, really—on our bed. Are you going home soon?"

"Soon enough. How's your temperature?"

I swore. "I forgot to bring the thermometer today." So much for tracking my basal body temperature.

"Well, either way I'll see you later. If you know what I mean."

Oh, yes. I knew what he meant.

Bette was already in the distribution shed when I returned, her lower lip clamped between her teeth as she carefully weighed out her portion of basil.

"I see a caprese salad in our future," I said by way of greeting from the doorway. "How about you?"

She looked up, startled. Then she smiled. "Maybe I could buy some of your homemade mozzarella?"

"Oh, I think we could work out a trade of some kind. Listen, would you do me a favor?"

A now-what? look crossed her face.

I laughed. "Don't worry. Nothing like earlier. I was just wondering if you could stick around for a few minutes while I run up to the house. And if any other members come in ask them to wait for me? I'm trying to make sure everyone gets a look at both of those pictures."

"So no one's identified your mystery woman?" She quickly counted out tomatoes and placed them carefully in her bike pannier, on top of the acorn squash.

I shook my head.

"Well, I'd love to stick around and help, but I'm afraid I'm meeting a friend for dinner. I'm late as it is. Sorry, Sophie Mae." She topped the tomatoes with the herbs, and, looking harried, gave me an apologetic wave and rushed out to fasten the pack onto her cruiser.

Fine. I found the marker Allie used to list the share particulars and added a note on the bottom of the dry erase board. *Must talk with all members. Please wait. Be right back.*

But about halfway to the farmhouse, another car pulled in. I turned around and retraced my steps down the dirt road as Daphne Sparks got out of her Jetta. She waved when she saw me and went inside. When I walked in she was standing with her hands on her hips, looking at the sign.

"Hi, Sophie Mae!" She gestured toward my note. "Any idea what that's all about?"

She was tall, in her early twenties, with straight, blue-black hair and bright green eyes. I wasn't surprised she'd joined the Turners' venture, as she was finishing up her horticulture studies at Evergreen Community College, and I knew for a fact she had a special affinity for plants, especially herbs.

The hope that I'd really discover the bird lady's identity had given way to simple stubbornness. I removed the photos from the envelope and laid them in a clear space next to the peppers. "This is what it's about. You know the woman we found yesterday? These are pictures of her. I'm trying to find out if any of the CSA members recognize either one of them." By now my rote words tumbled out without much expectation.

Hesitantly, she approached. "Do I have to look?"

"Well, I can't make you. But if you know her, wouldn't you want to help find her killer?"

She blanched. "Killer?"

"It looks like it. But the police don't even know who she is."

Another few beats, then she took another step toward me. "Okay. I'll look. But karma will catch up with whoever did that to her. You know that, right?"

Karma might be a bitch, but I was too impatient to wait for her.

"Oh, my God."

I held my breath.

"You need to show these to Nate." She held up both pictures.

"Who is she?" I asked, trying to remain calm.

Daphne shook her head. "I could be wrong—I never saw her up close. But Nate will know for sure."

TWELVE

I SWIPED MY NOTE off the dry-erase board, grabbed up the photos and trotted out the door, tossing a "Thank you!" over my shoulder. But Daphne was in for a pound now, and hurried to join me. We practically ran to the house—well, I practically ran. My companion was tall enough to outstride me by half. At a little after seven o'clock, the sun was lower in the sky, and increasing cloud cover created a false twilight. The motion sensor light over the front door flicked on as we neared.

Daphne pulled at my arm. "Nate's probably in his trailer."

We went around the side of the house. The silver Airstream gleamed, and cheery yellow light spilled through the red gingham curtains that covered the open windows. The savory smell of cooking onions drifted out on the sound of rattling pans.

"*How could you?*" The harsh feminine shriek from inside the trailer stopped us in our tracks.

Daphne and I exchanged looks. Her shoulders drooped.

"You know I'll never give up. And I'll never give up because I know you really do love me."

A low male murmur in response.

My heartbeat quickened.

"Remember how much fun we used to have?" The voice cajoled. Yick.

Another murmur.

I darted a look at my companion, but she just rolled her eyes and started for the trailer. Clutching at her arm, I pulled her back to the corner of the house. I held my finger to my lips and gave a slight shake of my head.

"What?" she whispered.

"We don't know what's going on in there," I whispered back, reaching into my pocket. "I'm calling the cops."

Confusion mixed with anger on her face, and she shook off the hand which still gripped her elbow. "What for? It's just Hallie."

"Are you sure?"

"Of course. Who do you think it is?"

Oh, I don't know. Another potential victim?

"Why is she so upset?" I asked.

Daphne looked at me like I was missing a few bolts. "Because she's Hallie. And she's out of her freaking mind when it comes to Nate."

Now I was confused. "I didn't even know they were dating."

"They're not."

I rubbed my forehead. "Then why—"

"No!" exclaimed the voice from the trailer. "You need to remember how it was between us. It can't be that way between you and Daphne. It just can't. You wouldn't be cheating on her if it was."

"That won't work," Nate's words were clear now. "You're not going to break us up with your lies. I've had enough. Please just go back home, and leave me alone." His voice cracked on the last three words. "Please."

"You creep!" Hallie shouted.

Daphne took off, running toward the trailer. I was right behind her.

But before she could get to the door, it opened. Hallie stumbled out of the trailer. Her face was crimson with anger, and tears shone from dark, wild eyes. She snarled at Daphne, pushing her roughly out of the way, and ran past me to the house. The back door to the farm house slammed behind her.

"I thought she was going to stop that nonsense," Daphne said from behind me.

I turned to find Daphne had gone into the trailer, and now she and Nate were thoroughly wrapped around each other. She was about four inches taller than he was, the crown of her head almost touching the low ceiling. His baby blues rose and looked at me over her shoulder.

"Er," I said, and stepped into the cramped interior of the trailer.

Blushing, Daphne let go of him. He was red, too, and shuffled his feet. "Hi, Sophie Mae. Did you, uh, did you hear any of that?" He gestured vaguely toward the farm house.

I nodded and waited expectantly. Sometimes if you just kept you mouth shut other people feel compelled to fill the silence.

Nate broke first. "See, Hallie seems to think she's, well, in love with me." His color deepened. He looked at Daphne, who looked disgusted. "She's not, of course," he rushed on. "Or if she is, it's not my fault. We went out for a while, when she first came to stay with Tom and Allie, but she was way too intense for me."

Daphne took over. "Nate broke it off with her. Said he wanted to stay friends." Her expression betrayed what she thought about that.

"I figured we live too close to be enemies," he said in a quiet voice.

She stroked his arm. "I know, I know." Her attention returned to me. "But Hallie didn't take it well. It's been over a year, and she still wants to get back together." She shot an affectionate look at Nate. "We've been dating for four months, and it makes her *crazy*." Daphne paused, then shrugged. "She really hates my guts. Do you know she followed us to the theater in Monroe last night? Sat right behind us. God, I could have killed her."

Interesting word choice. At least I knew where Hallie had been the night before when Barr had brought out the picture.

"We had it out in the parking lot afterward," Daphne continued. "I really thought she'd back off after that, but *no*." Frustration and anger leaked out of every word.

"You 'had it out'?"

"Oh!" She shook her head. "Nothing physical or anything. I just told her in no uncertain terms to lay off of Nate and me. She'd already tried to convince me Nate was seeing someone else." She glanced at him. "Which is why I brought Sophie Mae to see you, honey."

He looked confused.

I was equally bewildered. This drama had something to do with the bird lady?

"Show him, Sophie Mae."

Gesturing Nate toward me, I took out the pictures. They looked pretty ratty by now, scuffed and bent and smudged by all the fingers they'd been through. And after a horrible night's sleep and a long day, I was tired as all get out. Without preamble, I shoved them at him and stood back to watch his face.

He blinked at the two pieces of paper in his hands. Held them closer, his gaze flickering between them, and took a deep breath. "Oh," he said. Daphne hovered at his side.

"Do you recognize one of those?" I asked.

He nodded.

"Which one?"

Nate blinked a few more times, and I realized he was holding back tears. "Both."

Daphne put her arm around his shoulders, radiating sympathy. "It's the woman they found yesterday. When I saw the picture ... it's her, isn't it?"

He nodded again.

I couldn't contain myself. "Who? Nate, what's her *name*?"

He looked up at me, grief rolling off him in waves. "It's Darla. Darla Klick."

THIRTEEN

If there was ever a time when a bracing drink was in order, this was it. Nate's fingers curled around a glass of Jack Daniels, Daphne opted for a vodka tonic, and I sipped Johnny Walker from a shot glass with a picture of Elvis on the side.

The young Elvis. The thin Elvis. Funny how people changed.

The interior of the airstream trailer seemed bigger than it looked from the outside, but it was still cramped. A built-in table flipped down from the wall, but most of the furniture crammed into the small space looked like something out of a college dorm—wicker papasan chair in one corner, bean bag chair in another, and rough shelves made from cinderblocks and two-by-eight lumber. A futon functioned as both sofa and bed. Nate's half-cooked kale stir-fry languished in a wok on the two-burner stove.

I sat in the papasan chair, feet curled underneath me. The lovebirds sat side-by-side on the futon.

And Nate told me about Darla.

"We grew up together on Camano Island. Under sort of strange circumstances, actually. See, our parents were throwbacks, hippies into the back-to-the-land movement, only a few years late."

"She was your *sister*?" I interrupted, stunned.

"Oh! No. Different sets of parents. We were neighbors, if you could call the other people in your commune your neighbors. It was more like a huge extended family, all working together. There was a central kitchen, and everyone shared in the gardens and taking care of the animals. There was a one-room school, and all us kids went there. The parents took turns teaching us. Kind of like home schooling, but centralized."

"Doesn't it sound wonderful?" Daphne breathed.

Ah, the romance of youth. "I bet it was a lot of hard work," I said.

Nate nodded. "Oh, sure. But it was fun, too, at least the way I remember it." He took a deep breath. "Darla was my very best friend for nine years."

"I'm so sorry," I said.

He didn't seem to hear me. "When I was eighteen and Darla was seventeen, the man who owned the land sold it to a big corporation."

"And you all had to leave?" I asked.

"There's a resort there now," he said.

"How many families were involved in this commune?"

"About a dozen, give or take. People would come and go. And you didn't have to be a family to join us. A lot of single people were interested in belonging to a big community." He paused, looking into a distance that wasn't there.

Was he remembering the past, or thinking of the future?

Daphne nudged him. "Tell her about Darla."

"Right." I reined my imagination back in. "You stayed in contact with her?"

"For a while. But soon we lost touch, and I didn't see her for years and years. It turned out part of that time she was working in Alaska on some grant project."

"She was into birds, right, honey?" Daphne said.

"How do you know so much about her?" I asked her.

She scowled. "Hallie tracked me down one day about a week ago. I was out hoeing around the pumpkins. She just had to tell me about this 'other woman' Nate was seeing."

I looked at Nate.

He sighed. "Hallie likes to keep tabs on me, which isn't hard to do since this trailer is in her backyard. So she saw Darla come to see me. Darla was between assignments, and living with her parents in Arlington. She tracked me down through some mutual friends and gave me a call. I invited her to come see the farm. I opened the door, and there was my old friend after all those years. She'd lost weight and was in great shape—I'd never seen her look so hot."

Now I looked at Daphne.

Other than a slight flare of her nostrils, she ignored his commentary. "By the time Hallie saw fit to tell me about this new woman Nate was seeing, he'd already filled me in about Darla. About what good friends they were and how happy he was to see her again." She twisted to meet his eyes. "And about their … past. What a sad, sad story."

Nate offered a grimace. "I wish you could have met her, Daffy. You would have really liked each other."

"So you never actually saw her?" How had Daphne recognized the photos then?

"I did see her, but she was in the parking lot. She and Nate had been catching up and she was leaving. Nate pointed her out to me and said what he did just now. That we would really like each other. So when I saw the pictures, I was pretty sure they were of Darla. I knew Nate could tell you for certain."

"I think Darla lived in Cadyville for a time, maybe four or five years ago," I said.

His forehead creased. "I was in Oregon then. I moved around a lot after the commune folded. I was under the radar much of that time, working for cash on ranches and farms all over the West. It wasn't until I learned Tom was starting a CSA farm that I realized how much I missed this little corner of the world. When he offered me a job, I jumped at the chance."

We all fell silent, thinking about how Nate and Darla had finally managed to cross paths. When I eventually spoke, it was almost to myself. "So why did someone kill her?"

Nate passed his hand over his face and shook his head.

Daphne gave him a peck on the cheek. "Don't worry. Sophie Mae will find out what happened to her."

I hauled my behind out of the chair, awkward as all get-out. Now I remembered why papasans had gone out of style. "No promises. But knowing her identity is the first step in finding out more." I slipped on my shoes. "I'll pass on what you told me to the police. I'm sure they'll want to talk to you."

Nate stood. "Of course. Tell Barr I'll be available whenever he needs me. I want to find out who killed Darla as much as anyone."

As I stepped outside the door, I asked, "So how do you know Tom?"

"From the commune. He and Allie were one of the last couples to join before we had to leave the island."

I stared. "He knew Darla?"

Slowly, Nate nodded. "He and Allie both did."

Now I felt my own nostrils flare. "They both out and out lied to me."

Daphne's eyes widened, and she gripped the edge of the futon where she still sat. "Why would they do that?"

Wariness crept onto Nate's face. "Oh, no."

"Oh, no, *what*?" My patience was worn paper thin.

He closed his eyes and shook his head. "Don't jump to conclusions, Sophie Mae. They're just trying to protect the farm."

Well, now I not only knew who the murder victim was, but had a whole pile of possible suspects, too.

If Hallie "loved" Nate so much she was willing to stalk him and Daphne on a movie date, was she capable of doing worse? After all, she'd thought Nate was seeing Darla on the side. But in that case, wouldn't she have gone after Daphne first?

And what about Daphne? She seemed understandably irked by Hallie's histrionics and interference with her relationship, but not overly concerned. It sounded like she'd stood up for herself, and apparently for Nate as well, in the movie theater parking lot. She didn't seem concerned about Darla, or Hallie's allegations that Nate was cheating, either. Daphne was even more Zen than Meghan in some ways.

I tried to put myself in her position. If Barr came home and said he'd run into his best childhood friend and that friend happened to be female, would I be jealous? I liked to think not, especially as his ex-wife had already surfaced in a very unpleasant way early in our relationship. Nothing could top that. Besides, I trusted Barr. I couldn't fault Daphne for trusting Nate as well.

But what if she didn't? What if that was an act? After all, Nate had sat right in front of both of us and described his old friend as "hot." It was a stretch, but while Hallie might go after Daphne as a rival, Daphne might see Nate's old friend as a rival. I had a hard time wrapping my brain around all of it, however, mostly because Nate himself didn't seem like the type to elicit such strong emotion.

Yet I'd witnessed exactly that from Hallie.

Sheesh.

All this flew through my mind as I walked around to the front of the farmhouse. Before going home, I wanted to brace the Turners about Darla Klick.

Allie answered the door, took one look at my face and said, "Oh ..." She sighed and stepped back. "You'd better come in."

I remembered my promise to be careful. "I'd rather stay out here, if you don't mind."

Her forehead creased in puzzlement. "Dinner's on the stove. I take it you found out about Darla?"

"Why didn't you tell me?" I couldn't keep the irritation out of my voice. I'd worked all day trying to figure out who the dead woman was, and the Turners had known all along. "More importantly, why didn't you tell Barr?"

She glanced inside. "Clarissa? Clarissa! Turn off the stove, okay?" She came out to the small porch and closed the door behind her. We sat down on the top step.

Allie turned to me with apprehension. "I'm sorry, really I am. She looked so different in the picture Barr showed us, and it had been so long. I couldn't be positive."

I shook my head. "I don't believe you. You knew her better than that."

"Not that well." She licked her lips. "And yet too well. What did Nate tell you?"

"That you and Tom were part of the commune where he and Darla grew up."

"Right. But only for six months before it all disbanded. By then Darla was falling apart, and she was gone a lot."

"College?"

"Rehab."

I felt my eyebrows climb my forehead. Nate hadn't said anything about substance abuse.

"Poor thing was a real mess," Allie went on. "Problems with drugs and alcohol ... and promiscuity. At least that's what I heard. And one time I caught her ..." She swallowed convulsively. "... I caught her with Tom."

Oooohhh. I struggled to keep my face expressionless. It didn't work.

"No, it's not like that," Allie said, rushing her words now. "She was kissing him, yes, and pawing at his clothes, but he was trying to stop her. It was awful, caused a big stink. We were newcomers while her parents were part of the group who originally founded the whole place. Something had happened, some kind of accident, and they knew all about it and blamed her behavior on that. I wasn't sorry when the owner sold the property we were all on. There was even talk of trying to find another piece of land together, but by then I didn't want any part of it."

A weariness settled around her slumped shoulders, but I could tell some of the anxiousness had lifted. Lying was a stressful business.

"Did you really think we wouldn't find out eventually?" I was still peeved.

She took a deep breath. "Tom and I just ... we thought there might be a way to save the farm."

I leaned forward. "Allie, did you kill Darla Klick?"

"Of course not!"

"Did Tom?"

"No! But once the police found out about that old connection we knew everyone would turn suspicious eyes on us. We thought if we could only stay under the radar, Barr would find who killed her, and people would still want to be part of the farm."

I just looked at her.

She held up a hand. "I know. Stupid."

More like desperate.

"Did you see her here?" I asked.

"Never. I didn't have the faintest clue she was anywhere near Cadyville."

"She sought out Nate," I said.

Allie nodded. "I'm not surprised. Apparently they were awfully close as kids."

And yet they'd fallen out of touch.

The door opened behind us, and we craned around to see Clarissa standing in the doorway. She looked right at me, then turned to her mother as if I didn't exist. "Hallie's crying. And something's burning in the kitchen. It smells really bad."

Allie launched to her feet. "Didn't you turn off the stove like I asked?"

"My nails are wet." She twiddled her fingers at her mother, who rushed past her into the house.

I stood. Clarissa leaned a hip against the doorframe and considered me. She wore a mini-skirt with high heels and a skimpy top that would have suited a street walker but merely looked sad on her scrawny, little-girl torso. Bright pink lipstick gleamed on her lips, and her light brown hair was gathered into a high ponytail on top of her head.

"I have to be going," I said. "Will you tell your mom?"

"Sure."

Unless her wet nails got in the way.

FOURTEEN

At home everyone was seated around the big butcher block table, chatting over the remnants of falling-apart baby-back ribs, baked beans, and tomato salad. A flaky apple strudel sat cooling on the counter. Brodie didn't even spare me a glance, all his attention devoted to willing a tasty morsel to drop right in front of him. Conversation ebbed and all heads turned to me when I walked into the kitchen and sat down beside Erin.

Barr opened his mouth to speak, but I cut him off.

"Darla Klick."

He closed his mouth and raised one eyebrow then smiled slow like he does when he's impressed. Kelly looked confused and then got it and began to grin. Erin said, "Who?"

But Meghan's head jerked up in recognition. "That name's on my short list."

"Well, your list is even shorter now. Nate Snow identified her." I added a scoop of beans to my plate. Bless her heart, Meghan had included plenty of bacon.

Barr pushed the salad bowl toward me. "Nice job, darlin'. How does he know her?"

"Apparently they grew up together, out on Camano Island. Some kind of a commune." I snagged a piece of tomato drowning in vinaigrette.

Kelly looked skeptical. "Really?"

I licked barbecue sauce off my fingers. "Yep. Sounds like kind of a weird upbringing. Bunch of families, home schooling, living off the land—at least that's the way Nate described it. And guess who else was part of the commune?"

"Who?" Meghan asked dutifully.

"Tom and Allie Turner."

Barr sat back and whistled. "So they lied to me last night."

"Well, I talked to Allie about that."

"Sophie Mae!" Meghan protested.

My husband pressed his lips together but didn't say anything.

"I was careful—didn't even go into the house. But I'd spent hours bracing the other members, not to mention the whole business of making Bette fuss with that photo this morning, all because those two were too afraid to admit that they knew Ms. Klick." I took a bite of molasses-laced beans and nearly moaned.

"Is that what Allie told you?" Barr asked. "That they were afraid?"

"More or less." I glanced at Erin. "I'll fill you in on the rest after dinner."

She scowled at me. "I'm twelve years old, Sophie Mae. I think I can handle it."

"A fact you seem to be bringing up a lot," Meghan said.

Erin pushed back from the table. "Fine. I'm going in my room and shutting the door and turning on my music so you can talk all you want without having to worry about offending my tender ears." She stomped out of the room. We heard the music come on, and then the door closed.

"Stop gritting your teeth," I said to Meghan.

Kelly held up a finger and quietly stood. Our eyes met, and I nodded.

"So then Allie said after the commune broke up they all ran away and joined the circus." I spoke a little louder than necessary.

Meghan's forehead creased, and then understanding dawned. Barr looked amused as Kelly sidled to the doorway and peeked around the edge.

"Gotcha."

"Kellleeeeee! Geesh, what a sneak." Erin's voice came from the other side of the wall.

"Takes one to know one," I called.

This time when her bedroom door closed, she was on the inside.

Barr laughed, and Meghan shook her head. As long as Erin had been so kind as to absent herself, I quickly filled them in on Hallie's behavior in Nate's trailer and Allie's tale of Darla at the commune, finishing with, "So Allie says she didn't really know her that well, and couldn't be sure that was her in the picture. But she sure remembered Darla accosting her husband."

My dear husband looked unconvinced. "You didn't talk to Tom?"

I shook my head. "Left that for you to do." I gnawed on a tender pork rib.

Barr sighed and looked at his watch. "Yeah. I guess I should. Nate, too. Save me a piece of strudel, 'K?" Within seconds he was dialing his phone. "Sergeant? Looks like the Jane Doe is named Darla Klick … Yeah … Sophie Mae did. I'm going out to talk to Nate Snow. He lives out at the Turner farm, and that's who identified her … right … next of kin. Let me know what you find out."

He grabbed his jacket, kissed me, and hurried out.

"Bug, come get some dessert," Meghan called. Miraculously, Erin responded, almost as if she was waiting for the summons. Maybe it was the strudel, or maybe she felt a little sheepish about trying to pull one over on us.

But I sat stunned. *Next of kin.* Darla hadn't just been Nate Snow's childhood friend and an ornithologist who took the time to talk to Erin about merlins. She was any number of other things: daughter, sister, maybe even wife and mother, though Nate hadn't said anything about her being married.

Which made me think about my parents and how they'd lost a son, how it had devastated them for years. How I'd lost a brother.

How I couldn't imagine losing a child. The thought bolted through my overtired brain before I could marshal any defense. What was I thinking? Maybe Barr and I were just fine without progeny.

Together, mother and daughter began clearing dishes. I watched as they stood hip-to-hip at the sink. Meghan leaned down and murmured something into Erin's hair, and Erin giggled.

I turned my head to find Kelly looking at me as if he knew exactly what I was thinking. A slow smile spread across his face. That was why Barr and I were trying to get pregnant. There is always the threat of sorrow in life, but there is also real joy to be gleaned from our short years on earth if we're brave enough to go after it.

I helped with the cleanup before leaving Meghan and Erin and Kelly to what was becoming more and more like regular family time. Down in my workroom, I worked on the books for a while, but my mind wasn't all that interested in invoicing and accounts. I did manage to order bulk ingredients for the new line of body oils before I hit the Internet.

Searching for "Darla Klick" netted me a professional page on a social network that I didn't belong to (who had the time for such things?) and a five-year-old reference in a research paper from the University of Alaska. I was just considering joining the social network despite my tendency to shy away from such things when I heard the door shut upstairs, voices, and soon after footsteps on the stairs from the kitchen.

I met Barr in the door to my office/storeroom. "That didn't take long."

"That's because no one is home at the farm."

My eyebrows rose. "I sure got the impression Nate, at least, was expecting you. Maybe he thought you'd talk to him tomorrow?"

Irritation flickered across his face. "Looks like I'll have to make the trip again." Then he grinned. "But maybe it's not so bad that I got home early."

I grinned back. "Are you thinking about a little dessert?"

"Yes, ma'am. And I'm not talking about apple strudel, either."

I slept hard and awoke refreshed shortly after dawn. No bad dreams—no dreams at all that I remembered. Apparently taking action had helped to assuage my horror over how Darla Klick had died.

A detail I hadn't shared with Nate or Daphne the night before.

Stretching like a cat, I turned toward the bedroom window. A hint of bright blue peeked around the edge of the curtain, and the sounds of chickens clucking contentedly to one another drifted in. Beside me, Barr stirred, and then he had his arm wrapped around me and was pulling me toward him.

"Feel like a little reprise?" he murmured in my ear.

I turned in his arms. "Someone's making up for lost time."

"Just trying to be efficient, is all."

"Well, by all means, then. In the name of efficiency and all."

An hour later I slipped a spatula under the potatoes browning on the stove. A few more minutes and they'd be perfect. A plate of sausages warmed in the oven, and I cracked eggs into a bowl of freshly snipped chives. Barr sat at the table sipping coffee.

I'd tried out the thermometer again before coming downstairs. 98.1°. My basal body temp chart might be flat lined, but I didn't care. I smiled over at my husband.

Meghan shuffled in, tying her bathrobe and yawning. A sleepy-looking Kelly followed right behind her, wearing the same clothes he'd had on yesterday. I raised my eyebrows and looked at my husband, who mirrored my expression, then ducked his head and took another sip of coffee.

"Good morning, you two." I grabbed three more eggs to add to the mix. The shells were differing shades of light green and blue, so I knew the Araucana hens, Molly and Emma, had laid them.

"Morning," they mumbled in unison.

"You're up bright and early. Sit down. Breakfast will be ready in a few minutes."

Soon we were digging in and making small talk, no one mentioning the elephant in the room. Meghan and Kelly had dated for well over a year, he'd uprooted his entire life and relocated to Cadyville so they could be together, and he spent nearly every evening at our house like one of the family. Yet to the best of my knowledge he'd never spent the *whole* night.

To the best of my knowledge. Just wait until I got Meghan alone.

"Any more interviews today?" I asked Barr.

He shook his head. "I'm going out to the farm first thing to talk to Nate."

"Fancy that. I was planning to head out there, too."

Meghan shot me a look.

"To finish a job I started for Tom yesterday," I said. "He wants the popcorn picked and stored so it can dry, and it's supposed to rain tonight."

Everyone at the table looked skeptical. Too bad.

Kelly looked at his watch and suddenly stood. "Oh! I've got to go. Gotta surveillance gig down in Seattle."

Meghan looked unhappy. He noticed and leaned down, wrapping his arm around her and kissing her on the neck. "Don't worry. I'll call you later." And he was out the door.

Meeting my housemate's eyes, I gestured toward Barr with my chin. "Welcome to the wait-and-worry club. You just have to trust that they'll be okay."

She pointed at me. "Thanks to you, I've been a member of that club for a long time."

Erin came in before I could respond. "Did I hear Kelly?"

Barr pushed back from the table. "I'll see you all later. Bye, hon."

"Bye," I said, but I followed him out to the hallway. Meghan was on her own.

FIFTEEN

I PARKED THE ROVER and got out. Though not yet eight o'clock, the sun had begun to warm the fields, and the air smelled of green leaves and rich earth. Barr hadn't arrived yet, no doubt snagged by station business. Pulling on a pair of gloves, I made my leisurely way to the tool shed. It was unlocked as always, and the garden cart sat right where I'd left it the night before.

I tugged it outside and down the path to the popcorn field. The thick rubber wheels bounced over rocks, making the removable slatted sides rattle in their moorings. The tower of compost rose in my peripheral vision to my left. I found myself veering toward it, cart still in tow. I stopped outside the police tape, one end of which now flapped lazily in the breeze.

Unlike where I'd grown up in northern Colorado, August mornings and evenings in the Pacific Northwest were almost always crisp. Today was no exception, and the moist heat of decay wisped up from the pile. I could tell someone had given the whole thing a good toss since we'd discovered Darla. Was that a result of simple farm efficiency, or had the police been involved? It hadn't occurred to me until now that there might be someone else in there, but the possibility had no doubt crossed Barr's radar. I shuddered at the thought. In this case, no news was definitely good news.

I closed my eyes and tried to picture what the pile had looked like before Meghan and I had started digging up Darla. Had there been any indication she'd been moved there? Drag marks? Wheel tracks? Foot prints? Why hadn't I paid more attention?

Oh. Right. Dead person. Very distracting. Still, I should have been more observant.

Even if I couldn't remember anything specific it didn't mean Darla hadn't been killed elsewhere and transported to the burial site. Between the digging and the emergency personnel, the area had been thoroughly messed up with footprints.

Not to mention hoof and chicken prints.

Several red hens pecked and scratched at the newly turned earth. Another reveled in a dust bath, fluffing her feathers and preening. Arnold Ziffel, the young pig Meghan had shooed away from her gruesome discovery two days earlier, came running up to me, grunting like, well, like a pig. He nosed me, begging for scritchin's. I obliged with a good rub between his ears. He followed me back to the path, trotting behind the cart until I shut the gate to the fields and left him behind. A single pig could do serious damage to the limited crops if he got the chance.

Wind sighed through the cornstalks, and crows called from beyond my view despite the stuffed scarecrow with the battered straw hat that towered at the edge of the patch. A whiff of manure drifted by as I worked my way down a row of popcorn. I snapped off the ripe ears and gently placed them in the cart while thinking about what I'd learned last night. Nate knew Darla Klick from way back, and they'd been in contact since she moved to Cadyville. But he'd been circumspect about how they'd fallen out of touch in the first place, his eyes darting to the left as he remembered something he hadn't shared. Was it because his girlfriend was sitting right beside him? Had he and Darla been more than friends? Or did it have to do with her going off the deep end as Allie described? She'd said something about an accident everyone blamed Darla's dissolution on—and come to think of it, Daphne had referenced a "sad story" Nate had related to her. Were they both talking about the same thing?

Nate had a lot more questions to answer. I could hardly wait to hear what he'd tell Barr.

And then there was Daphne. She knew of Darla, and seemed to believe Nate about the whole friends-only thing. She didn't come across at all like crazy Hallie.

And what about Hallie? She'd seen Darla go into Nate's trailer. Did she really think he was cheating on his girlfriend? Or would Hallie see it as more cheating on her? Was she really that unstable?

Remembering the look on her face as she exited Nate's trailer, I had to admit it was possible.

And then there were Tom and Allie Turner. Once I'd confronted her with the lie, Allie had opened up rather quickly. Was an untoward advance on her husband at least a decade earlier enough for her to kill Darla? That seemed a stretch. But maybe the advance had been more than that. After all, Allie had already lied, so I had to take whatever she said now with a grain of salt.

A flurry of black wings exploded out of the corn in front of me. My heart bucked, and I squeaked in surprise.

Dang crows. Sheesh.

Taking a deep breath to calm my nerves, I reached for another ear.

What about Tom? Had he lied, as Allie had said, just to protect the farm? I remembered his reaction when we'd first found Darla had been simple disbelief. *This is some kind of joke, right?* I didn't know him that well, but I knew others who tried to deal with unpleasantness by simply wishing it away.

On the other hand, he could have suspected his wife had killed her and had lied to protect her.

Why on earth had I thought that finding out the bird lady's identity would simplify matters?

Ear-by-ear I filled the cart to the top. Mr. Ziffel had lost interest and wandered away from the gate by the time I returned to the farm stand. Barr's department car was parked next to the Rover now. No sign of him, though. My eyes and ears on high alert for any sign of activity, I unloaded the popcorn and spread it to dry. Two more full loads should do it, for a total of five, including the two I'd picked between talking to the other CSA members the afternoon before.

If Barr wasn't done talking to Nate by then I'd just have to come up with some other excuse to hang around the farm.

Not wanting to miss talking to my husband, I picked as fast as I could now. Finishing one row, I turned down the next. The cart snagged on something, and I gave it a hard yank, trusting its rugged construction. I certainly didn't expect it to upend, dumping all the popcorn on the ground.

"Darn it!" Hands on hips, I surveyed the damage. Took a deep, calming breath.

The cart looked fine, the corn unbruised. I righted it and scanned the ground to see what had caused the problem.

Oh, no.

No, no, no, no.

I covered my eyes with both hands. See no evil. But when I dropped them, the boot was still sticking out from between the stalks of corn.

At least Meghan could rest easy, because the bodies were back to cropping up on my watch. This time the boot had the Wolverine logo on the side, and it definitely didn't belong to a woman. It looked more like a work boot than a hiking boot, solid and heavy. Gently pushing apart the corn stalks revealed a denim-clad leg, then two pockets and the telltale straps of overalls criss-crossed over a green flannel shirt.

And above that, a brown ponytail stained with blood.

Oh, no.

Oh, Nate.

SIXTEEN

"Sophie Mae! Are you out here?" It was my husband. Nice timing.

"Over here," I croaked, then tried again. "Barr! Hurry!"

He came around the corner of the corn patch. His eyes lit up when he saw me, which made me feel a little better. "Nate still isn't back. Tom and Allie say he didn't show up at the farm house for breakfast this ..." he trailed off as he neared.

I nodded and rubbed both my eyes. "Yeah."

"Sophie Mae?" His voice held warning.

I sighed and pointed down at the boot.

He walked around the pile of spilled corn and stopped. Pulled apart the stalks like I had. Turned and looked at me.

"Well. Hell."

Barr pushed his way in and knelt by the body. Pressing the tips of his fingers on Nate's neck seemed an almost perfunctory gesture. Then he paused, staring at the ground, and his eyes widened.

Looking up at me, he said, "He's still alive."

First came the flashing lights and sirens. Then the well-oiled activities of the paramedics as they stabilized Nate's neck and moved him onto a collapsible gurney. A police prowler roared down the dirt drive, parked with a spray of gravel, and Sergeant Zahn sprang out. Immediately, he began to quiz Tom and Allie. I was too far away to hear either questions or answers, but they shook their heads and held up their palms, the very pictures of bewilderment. Barr gave me a quick squeeze before going to check in with the crime scene officers.

I stood out of the way in the door of the distribution shed and watched. Allie started to cry, and Tom put his arm around her shoulders. Could one of them have gone after Nate? It was possible he knew more about the encounter between Darla and Tom than either of the Turners wanted him to relate. On the other hand, if the discovery of a murder victim in their compost pile was bad, a second attack only made things worse for their CSA dream.

Finished with the Turners for the moment, Zahn walked over and stopped in front of me. He raised one eyebrow. "Really?"

I looked at the sky, silently invoking patience. "Hey, at least he's not dead."

"For now. Someone hit him pretty hard. Looks like they used a shovel."

"Just like Darla Klick. Did you find it?"

"Not yet. Listen, you're not some twisted serial killer who goes around offing people just so she can find the bodies, are you?"

I glared at him. "That's not funny."

"Sorry." He still appeared amused, though.

"Not one little, stinking bit funny."

"Okay, okay. Tell me what happened."

Well, that was easy. "I was picking corn. The cart ran into Nate's foot and turned over."

"And?"

"And nothing. Barr came looking for me right after that. You know everything else."

He passed a hand through his hair. "I wish that were true."

"At least you know who the Jane Doe is. Did you find any family?"

Zahn nodded. "Her parents in Arlington and an older brother in Mount Vernon, but they already knew she was dead."

"What! How could they?"

"Nate Snow went to see the parents last night after you talked with him. They said he wanted them to hear it from a friend instead of some stranger in a uniform. He knew Ms. Klick had been staying with them between work assignments."

"That's probably where he was when Barr came out here to talk to him," I breathed. "But where was everyone else last night?"

"The Turners said they all went out to eat. Something about an accident in the kitchen."

The burned dinner, partly my fault for insisting on staying outside to question Allie. I wondered if Clarissa had enjoyed her restaurant meal with her fresh manicure.

"Then when did this—" I made a sweeping gesture from the popcorn field to the ambulance. "—all happen?"

"Obviously after Nate got back from Arlington and before you started picking corn. We'll know more soon."

"All right. What do you want me to do?" I asked.

"Nothing." All trace of amusement had vanished from Zahn's demeanor.

"But you said—"

"Someone is going around hitting people in the head with a shovel. We have no idea who, no idea why, and no idea how he picks his victims."

I shivered.

Zahn continued. "You should stay away from here until we get it all figured out. I've already told Tom and Allie to stick close to each other and stay watchful, since they refuse to leave."

"Well, of course they wouldn't leave their own farm."

"Tom told me the volunteers who were coming in today canceled," Zahn said.

"The *Cadyville Eye* hit the streets this morning, so the word's out about the murder," I said. "People are scared, and this attack on Nate isn't going to help."

"Murder's not good for business," he agreed.

Hallie's bright red Camaro pulled up just as they were loading Nate into the ambulance. She stomped on the brake, sliding on the gravel, and boiled out of the driver's side almost before the car had stopped. A white-faced Clarissa gazed out the passenger window with wide eyes.

"What happened? Who is that?" Hallie demanded.

Tom touched her arm, but she pushed him away. Running to the gurney, she grabbed Nate's shoulders. Unconscious, he couldn't even fight her off.

"Ma'am! Please!" Two paramedics held her back.

Allie ran up and put both arms around her sister. She spoke in a low voice. Hallie's features turned to stone as tears streaked down Allie's face. Tom urged them toward the house. As they slowly walked away, he came back and opened Hallie's passenger door.

"Come on, honey."

Clarissa got out slowly. "Who died this time?" Gone was the attitude and sass.

Tom's voice was soft. "Nobody. But Nate's hurt. They're going to take him to the hospital."

"Is he going to be okay?"

I watched her father consider and then decide. "We don't know yet. He's hurt pretty bad."

She bit her lip, every inch a little girl, and he folded her into his long arms. After a few moments, they moved off toward the house together.

I turned to Barr. "I told you Hallie was kind of a nutcase about Nate, but I might not have conveyed how crazy she was acting last night. Yelling and screaming. Daphne says she's horribly jealous, even though she and Nate didn't have a very long relationship and it was over a year ago."

"Almost sounds like your old stalker."

I waved my hand. "Oh, he wasn't crazy. He was just lonely and young and awkward. A little therapy fixed him right up." Okay, that wasn't entirely true. But in a short amount of time my erstwhile stalker had matured considerably and was now attending the University of Oregon in Eugene. "Do you think Hallie could have done this? Hit him in a fit of rage?"

Barr gave me that look that said I was asking him to jump to conclusions before he was ready to even dip a toe into speculation.

"If she saw Darla around here she might have killed her out of jealousy, too."

"Sophie Mae ..."

"It completely fits, is all I'm saying. Hey, what about Daphne? She could be in real danger. And she doesn't know what happened to Nate. I'd better go tell her."

"No, *I'd* better go tell her."

"Why?"

"Because she's a suspect."

"And a possible victim," I insisted. "If Hallie went wacko enough to hit both Darla and Nate over the head, she might try it with his real girlfriend, too."

"True," Barr said. "I'll certainly warn her to be careful."

"And ask her a bunch of questions. I think I'd better go with you."

"Well ..."

"Go ahead and take her," Sergeant Zahn said from behind us. "Maybe Ms. Sparks will be more forthcoming with your bride along."

Barr smiled at me and shook his head. "I can't say he's wrong. Let's go."

I smiled back. "Can you drop me back here when we're done, or should I take my own car?"

"I'll drop you."

Glancing over my shoulder, I saw yellow tape cordoning off the popcorn field. All that bright ribbon around the farm lent an air of morbid festivity. I could only hope this was the last of it. I followed Barr to the parking lot.

As I was transferring my tote bag to his car, Allie and Tom came hurrying up from the house. She pulled a resistant Clarissa behind her. It was obvious they were making a beeline for us, so we waited, Barr almost tapping the pointy toe of his cowboy boot in impatience. Then I saw Tom was carrying a duffel bag, and felt a twist of dread.

It was bright pink.

Sure enough, when they reached us Allie said, "We have a huge favor to ask of you."

Clarissa glared at her mother. Then at me. Tom put his hand on her shoulder, but she'd regained her composure and shrugged it off.

"Honey," he said. "It's for your own good." Then he looked between Barr and me. "We were wondering if Clarissa could stay with you for a few days. Just until we know why two people have been attacked here on the farm. Her mother and I can't leave, of course, but we want her to be safe." He gave an apologetic grimace. "Clarissa doesn't know that many other girls, and she likes Erin a lot. Besides, we figure Detective Ambrose's house is bound to be one of the safest places in town."

I looked up at Barr. He looked down at me. We both looked at Clarissa, who refused to look at us.

Barr said, "I think that's a good idea. Do you have all your stuff, Clarissa?"

She sighed, long and hard. "I guess."

"Okay, then." I forced a bright note into my voice. "Erin's going to be so excited!"

Meghan, on the other hand, was going to kill me.

SEVENTEEN

Our surprise houseguest threw a potential monkey wrench into our plans. I called Meghan, but she didn't answer her phone. That likely meant she was with a client. I didn't know what the rest of her massage schedule was for the morning, either—our usual routine for keeping track of each other's coming and goings had gone right out the window as soon as people started getting whacked upside their heads.

"Dang it," I said under my breath. Retrieving my tote from the department's nondescript undercover sedan, I dropped my phone into it and turned to Barr. "Clarissa and I had better go straight to the house. I guess you're on your own with Daphne."

"How about I meet you at home," he said. "Meghan might just be in the backyard. Or Cyan can watch her."

"No one needs to watch me!" Clarissa protested. Her parents exchanged glances.

"We always watch each other at our house," I said firmly. "No one goes wandering off on their own, either. It's one of the rules." I emphasized the last word.

Tom looked relieved, but worry continued to crease Allie's forehead.

Clarissa's lower lip crept out. "Rules." Disgust dripped from the word. "Then where's Erin right now?"

"Clarissa, please don't be mad," Allie said. "Like Daddy said, it's for your own good."

Her daughter shrugged.

Oh, boy. The next few days were going to be fun. "We'll find out where she is when we get home." My smile didn't quite make it to my eyes, and my next words didn't sound quite as friendly as I'd hoped. "Now, get in the car."

She shot me a surprised look but climbed into the passenger seat of the Rover. I got in the other side and slid the key into the ignition. Tom tossed her duffel in the back and leaned his elbows on the open window frame beside her. "I don't want to hear that you've misbehaved. I want you to be polite and to do what you're told."

She opened her mouth, but he quickly shook his head. "No. You've been getting away with a lot around here lately, and it's going to stop. These folks are doing us a huge favor in order to keep you safe. You will not cop an attitude. You will be helpful and pleasant and do as you're asked. And you'll answer to me if I hear differently."

Clarissa gaped at her father.

"Tom …" Allie trailed off.

I realized how tired she looked, like the last few days had wrung the spark right out of her. She was an empty husk, unable to stand up to either her daughter or her husband. I had a sudden urge to hug her, while at the same time I wanted to shake some backbone into her.

But I didn't want to distract Clarissa after her father's admonitions. Best be on our way.

"Seat belt?" I asked.

Silent, she fastened it.

"All righty then. Here we go."

I waved at Tom and Allie. After a moment's hesitation Clarissa did, too.

* * *

At the house I pulled up behind a black Lexus. Barr's department car was across the street, but he had beaten me home and gone inside already. A blond-haired, blue-eyed guy who looked like he belonged on the cover of a torrid romance exited the front door, gave me a friendly nod, and slid into the Lexus. Clarissa and I got out of the Rover as it drove away.

"Who was *that*?" she asked.

"One of Meghan's clients, I'm sure." For the first time I wondered whether Kelly ever minded that his girlfriend made her living by rubbing naked people. She was a consummate professional, of course, devoted to making people feel better. And she loved her work, so much that she'd given up her career as a lawyer in order to do it. But I didn't know how understanding I'd be if Barr spent a few hours every day running greasy hands over other women.

Did that make me sexist? Oh, well.

We found Barr in the kitchen, rummaging through the cupboard. It was already lunchtime.

"Are you hungry?" I asked Clarissa. She shook her head, stopped, shrugged one shoulder.

"I'll make some sandwiches," Barr said. "Meghan's in her office."

I nodded and took a deep breath. My best friend wasn't fond of surprises. Bracing, I went to update her on the morning's developments.

She was sitting at her desk jotting notes in a client file when I walked in.

"Um," I said.

She looked up. "Um?" Then she really focused on my face and her expression became wary. "Um, what." Her voice was flat.

"Um, you know how I was out at the farm this morning?"

"Yes."

"And how Barr was going to talk to Nate Snow?"

"Yes."

"Well, I found Nate. Someone hit him in the head. Zahn said it was probably a shovel. Anyway, I found him in the popcorn, unconscious, and the ambulance took him to the hospital. I don't know how bad it is, but it doesn't sound good. I want to go with Barr to tell Daphne. She's going to be pretty upset—unless she's the one who hit him, of course. Barr says she's a suspect. Anyway,

Clarissa came home with me, and she's going to stay with us until we find out who's attacking people at the farm."

Meghan blinked.

I barreled on. "Tom and Allie asked if she could—they're scared, you know—and Barr thought it would be a good idea, so I said okay and now she's in the kitchen and Barr is making sandwiches. Do you want one?"

She stared at me, and I could sense her careful deep breaths as she considered all the information I'd thrown at her. "Yes, please," she finally said.

"Where's Erin?"

"At Zoe's."

"Okay. So we're going to grab a bite and then Barr and I are heading over to Daphne's. Do you have another client soon?"

She took another breath. "You are amazing. I love you to death, but sometimes I just want to strangle you."

"I know."

"But I can see why the Turners would want Clarissa to stay somewhere else for a while. We'll make it work." She stood.

I gave her a quick hug. "You're getting better at rolling with the punches."

"Or better at faking it." She flipped the file on her desk closed. "I don't have another client until three o'clock. Can you be back by then?"

"Absolutely."

A pile of sandwiches awaited us in the kitchen. Peanut butter and different kinds of preserves. Clarissa nibbled on the corner of one, and Barr was slugging a glass of milk. It didn't look as if they were having much of a conversation. I threw a look at Meghan that was part gratitude and part apology and opened the door at the head of the stairs. I heard a giggle below.

"Girls? There are sandwiches up here if you're hungry."

"Thanks!" Cyan called. "We'll be right up."

At least I'd brought in some reinforcements for Meghan. Grabbing half a sandwich dripping with cherry jam and wrapping it in a paper towel, I raised my eyebrows at Barr.

"I've eaten," he said. "Let's go."

"Is there a plan?" I asked around a big sticky bite of sandwich.

Barr puttered along at the sedate Cadyville speed limit of twenty-five miles an hour. "Nah. We're pretty good at this by now."

I sat back, pleased at his words. I was not so pleased, however, that I hadn't thought to bring anything to drink. All that peanut butter made me want to lick the roof of my mouth over and over like a dog.

And when I reached for Barr's water bottle it was, of course, empty.

Great.

The last time I'd been to Daphne Sparks' apartment her roommate had been murdered. It turned out they hadn't exactly been best friends, so she'd been able to weather the bad news fairly well. Still, it's disturbing to know someone you lived with died at the hand of another. Nate wasn't dead, of course, and they didn't live together, but I suspected this time Daphne wouldn't respond with such aplomb.

Barr pulled into the parking lot of a twelve-plex on the corner of Maple and Pine Streets. It was painted a peachy orange with green and maroon trim. Each balcony railing was lined with a long planter box. A profusion of red petunias tumbled from one, another held white geraniums and purple verbena, yet another boasted spiky grasses surrounded by dark purple and lime-green sweet potato vine. I was pleased to see that two renters had filled their tiny growing spaces with cherry tomatoes, tiny peppers, and baby lettuce. And one, on the second floor at the end, spilled over with all manner of herbs.

We got out, and I pointed at the apartment with the herb farm. "That's Daphne's." She lived alone, having given up on roommates after the last fiasco.

"If she's not here, she's probably in class," I said. Then it occurred to me she might have gone to the Turner farm. I crossed my fingers, hoping she hadn't.

My flip-flops flip-flopped up the wooden steps. Barr knocked on the metal door. Within seconds Daphne flung it open. Even taller than my husband, she towered over me.

She greeted us with, "What's wrong?" Her porcelain skin had taken on a new dimension of pale.

"Can we come in?" Barr asked.

She stepped back from the door with alacrity, gesturing us inside. "It's about Nate, isn't it?"

"Why do you say that?" Barr said, all official-like as we entered the apartment.

Oh, brother. Couldn't he see the frantic worry in her eyes?

"I've been trying to call him all morning, but he hasn't answered. He never does that. And he was supposed to call me last night and didn't. I even called the farm a while ago, but Hallie answered." She made a face. "She hung up on me!"

"What time was that?" Barr asked.

"About ten. I've already skipped two classes. I was about to go out there." She turned to me. "Sophie Mae? Do you know what's going on?"

I glanced at Barr, then back at her. "Let's sit down." That seemed to worry her even more, and I put my hand on her arm. She looked down at it like she didn't know what it was.

"Nate's in the hospital," I said.

Slowly, she sank down onto the overstuffed sofa. I sat beside her. Barr remained standing, looking around at the profusion of medicinal and culinary plants that inhabited every horizontal surface. The air vibrated with herbal scents—lavender and rosemary the most pungent. I only hoped they would calm her now.

"What happened?" she asked, obviously dreading the answer. "Did she hurt him?"

"Who?" Barr asked before I could open my mouth.

Daphne looked up at him. "Hallie." Her attention switched to me. "You saw how she was last night."

"I did," I said slowly.

"Well, what does he say?"

I could feel Barr watching. Well, this was why I'd insisted on coming. "Nate couldn't tell us what happened. See, he was struck on the head."

A sharp intake of breath.

"But he's okay?"

"Well, he's unconscious, honey."

She sprang to her feet. "I have to get to the hospital. Is it the one in Monroe?"

I stood, too. "Everett. Now slow down."

"But he needs me!" She ran into the bedroom and emerged with her purse. Keys jangled in her hand as she opened the front door.

"Daphne," I said.

She turned with an impatient look.

"You might want to take something to read."

She stared, then nodded once. "Yeah." She scooped up an organic chemistry textbook and a notebook from the sofa and jammed them into a backpack, followed by a laptop case. Slinging it over her shoulder, she picked up a small French lavender plant covered with blooms. In response to my questioning look she said, "It's good for the soul. Nate will need that."

Barr reached for the door. "Are you okay to drive?"

"I'll be fine," she said.

"Be careful," he said. "And watchful. Pay attention to your surroundings, and stay around other people as much as possible. And absolutely do *not* go out to the Turner farm."

That stopped her in her tracks. "What are you saying?"

"Be careful," he repeated.

I could see how he watched her, assessing, judging.

She took a shaky breath. "Are you going to arrest Hallie?"

"We're still investigating the crime. Crimes," he amended.

Frustration and anger pinched her features. "She'll be sorry if she comes after me."

So much for relying on karma to take care of business.

"Um, do you mind if I get a quick drink of water?" I asked.

"Knock yourself out. Just make sure that's locked before you go?" She indicated the knob in Barr's hand and then clattered down the stairs to her VW Jetta without waiting for an answer.

As the engine started up and the car exited onto Maple toward Second Street, Barr turned and looked at me. "Nice job."

"You mean telling her about Nate before you had a chance to ask her any questions? Sorry." I threaded my way to the open kitchen at the back of the apartment. I found a glass, ran cold tap water into it, and gulped it down. Bliss.

He followed. "No, I mean gaining her verbal permission to be in her apartment without her being here."

But I was concentrating on washing down the sticky peanut butter sandwich. When his words sank in, I poked my husband in the ribs with my index finger.

He flinched.

"Oh, come on," I said. "Do you think she faked all that?"

Brown eyes blinked slowly down at me. "Not really."

"Not really? So you think she might have? Why? What possible motive would that poor girl have to hurt her boyfriend?"

"The same one the woman she accused—Hallie—would have. Jealousy."

My lips parted. "So you think she faked her reaction just now? That she hit him in the head with a shovel herself, after doing the same thing to Darla Klick, all because she believes Nate and Darla were old flames?"

"Or maybe not-so-old flames."

I shook my head. "It's possible, I suppose. Seems to me like she's the only sane one in the bunch, though, especially after talking with her and Nate last night." Though come to think of it, she had been strangely eager to tell me Nate knew Darla. Had she been trying to throw suspicion on him for something she had done? Was she really that clever . . . and evil?

"And if she was the one who hurt him, should she even be at the hospital with him?" I asked Barr, who was now circling the apartment, looking everywhere but not touching. "Oh, wait a minute. Seriously? You're searching her apartment?"

He hesitated, gazing with tangible longing at the closed drawers in a desk in the corner.

"Lord love a duck. Do you think Daphne would leave a police detective in her apartment if she was hiding something nefarious here?"

The corners of his lips turned up. "You may be right. Criminals can be pretty stupid, though."

I didn't think Daphne was at all stupid. That didn't mean she wasn't hiding something, mind you, but I doubted it would be in her apartment.

"Okay, then. WWZD?" I asked.

His look was quizzical.

"What would Zahn do?"

That produced a sigh. "He'd get a warrant." Suddenly he reached out and tousled my already messy hair.

"Stop that!"

Grinning, he opened the door again and stepped outside. "Funny that you'd be the one to talk me out of tossing the place. Usually I'd be the one warning you off."

I followed him out. The latch snicked into place, and he tested the knob to make sure it locked.

As we went down the steps I tried to think why I hadn't wanted to jump in with both feet. I'd searched other places with no qualms. But this felt different, despite the fact that my husband the detective had been in favor of it. Why?

Barr started the engine.

I fastened my seat belt. I liked Daphne, and truly believed she was upset about Nate. Deep down, I didn't think she'd hurt him, at least not with a shovel. But I had to admit I could be off the mark. In the end it came down to the simple feeling that going through her things would have been … wrong.

Okay, so I had a conscience. I liked to think I always had, but apparently so much contact with death and grief and tragedy in the last few years had gradually thinned my skin when it came to moral dilemmas. In a way, I was glad. But it could also mean Kelly—and Barr and Zahn—were all wrong about my investigative abilities now.

Maybe I'd lost my edge.

EIGHTEEN

It was just before two o'clock when Barr dropped me at home and headed back to the cop shop. He promised to call if they got any news about Nate's condition. I strode up the walkway with purpose. It was all I had to fill the void left by the pile of unanswered questions about the events at the farm. There were a lot of reasons to kill someone. I'd personally known sociopathic negligence, greed, desire, fear for a loved one, simple anger, self-defense, and unadulterated ego to drive murderers. Given the dynamic of Hallie/Nate/Daphne/Darla or even Allie/Tom/Darla, all I could come up with was jealousy.

Would I ever be willing to kill for Barr?

Maybe. To save his life, say—but not out of jealousy.

Inside, I veered toward the kitchen, ready to go down to the basement and get some work done. I always felt better when I had a handle on tasks, when things were organized and items checked neatly off my to-do list. But then I saw Clarissa out of the corner of my eye and changed my mind.

She was sitting on the sofa in the living room, all alone. No television on, no books. Just sitting there.

I stopped and leaned against the arch that opened from the entryway into the living room. "Hey."

Her head jerked up in alarm.

"Didn't you hear me come in?"

"No."

Stepping into the room, I joined her on the sofa. "Whatcha doing?"

"Nothing." Her fingers twisted in her pink skirt. Knobby knees poked out from below it. She looked up at me with big eyes, and for the first time I saw they were deep blue.

"Where's Meghan?" I asked.

"She came and told us she had a, a drop-in or something."

That did happen sometimes, though I was surprised she'd leave Clarissa all alone out here to give a massage.

Wait a minute. "Us? Is Erin home?"

"Yeah."

My forehead wrinkled in surprise. "Then where is she?"

"In her bedroom with that Zoe girl."

Erin and Zoe had been friends since the first grade. But that didn't explain why Clarissa wasn't in there with them.

My perplexity must have shown because she said, "They were busy with some stupid 4-H project. A stupid organic garden."

I sat back and considered her. A white gauzy top rested on her skinny shoulders, and several beaded necklaces looped around her little neck. Diamond-look drops dangled from her ear lobes. She wasn't actually smaller than Erin, but she seemed smaller. Like somehow she lacked the same presence. I wondered how she'd talked Erin into defying her mother and going to the ice cream shop.

Then I remembered the cell phone. Erin's disobedience hadn't been about Clarissa at all.

"You don't like gardening?" I asked.

"Yuck. I don't like any of that stuff." Now her voice was stronger.

"You mean farm-type stuff?" I ventured.

"I hate that stupid farm."

"All of it? What about the pigs and chickens?"

"Especially the pigs and chickens!" Her jaw set. "They're dirty and nasty and ugly and I have to feed them all the time. I have to gather eggs, and the stupid hens peck at me and try to eat my jewelry. The pigs stink, and after I've been around them five minutes then *I* stink. Aunt Hallie's right. All animals are good for are eating."

"How about dogs?" I teased.

"They're not even good for that."

Wow. She really meant it. Or thought she did.

"How about people?"

She looked at me like I'd crawled out from under a rock. "You can't eat *people*."

I laughed—sort of. "But you can like them. You like people, right?"

"Some of them. I like Aunt Hallie."

"What about your parents?"

"They're the reason I have to live on that stupid farm. They're the reason we had to move away from home, why I had to change schools, why I had to leave all my friends."

Ouch. Unfortunately, if she kept up with this lousy attitude, she wouldn't be making very many new friends, either.

"They're the reason I can't have nice things like Aunt Hallie has." Her eyes filled with tears. "I like pretty things. I'm a girl, not a farm hand. But anything I wear at that stupid place gets dirty right away, and there isn't anyplace else to go." Clarissa was getting pretty worked up now. She yelled, "I hate this stupid little town. There aren't any good stores, and there's nothing fun to do."

Putting my hand on the girl's arm, I said, "Please lower your voice. Meghan's working."

Her tears spilled over.

I put my arm around her and pulled her into my shoulder. She strained against me for a moment, then relaxed and leaned against my side. I held her there, stroking her hair while she sniffled, without saying anything. This little girl was trying so hard to figure out who she was. My guess was that her friends had defined her before, but now they were gone. As much as I enjoyed volunteering at the Turners', I couldn't pretend to know what it would be like to live full-time on a farm, the stress of trying to make a living from one, or how that stress might affect a child in the house.

The only person she seemed close to was her crazy Aunt Hallie. That didn't bode well.

Her sniffles subsided, and we sat there for a while longer. Finally, I asked, "What do you like to do?"

"I like to shop," was her immediate reply. She peered up at me with red-rimmed eyes. "Do you like to shop?"

I grimaced. "Not really. Sorry."

"Why not?"

Why not indeed? "I think it's kind of boring."

She regarded me with a combination of disgust and amazement.

"You don't like working in the dirt, and I don't like shopping. There's nothing wrong with having different interests," I said.

One skinny shoulder rose and dropped. She looked at the floor. "I guess."

"I like your earrings, though."

Fear flickered through her eyes, and her fingers darted to the diamond drops. A little alarm went off in the back of my brain, and I leaned down for a closer look.

"Are those real diamonds?" I put some awe in my voice.

And as I watched, the fear turned hard. She pushed away from me. "So what if they are? Hallie has loads of nice stuff, and she lets me wear it sometimes."

"Does she know you have those right now?"

Her shrug was elaborate. "Maybe. Maybe not. After all, she's the one who told me it's better to apologize later than to ask permission first."

The alarm in my brain went clang, clang, clang.

"Otherwise you'll never get anything you want in life. That's what Hallie says."

Oh, boy. "What else does Hallie say?"

"Tons of stuff. She's really smart."

"How long has she lived with you?"

"I don't know. Back home she used to live down the street. Then she got divorced and came for a visit and decided she liked living with us so she stayed. And when we moved here, she came with us. My dad gets mad at her sometimes, but I hope she stays with us forever."

"What does your dad get mad about?" Though I had a pretty good idea.

"Silly stuff. Hallie should pay rent if she's going to live in our house, he says. Or she should work in the fields. She's like me though. She hates getting dirty, and she hates the animals. Only she's old, so he can't make her do things like he makes me." She sighed. "I can hardly wait to be old enough that I don't have to do what anyone tells me."

And she was already trying out her wings.

"Does Hallie have any kids of her own?" I asked. If so, her ex-husband must have custody—which would say a lot.

But Clarissa shook her head. "Nah. Mama said she wanted to but couldn't. She tells Daddy that's one of the reasons we have to be nice to her, 'cuz she's so sad about not having a baby."

I cringed inwardly. What if I couldn't get pregnant? Would I go through the rest of my life desperately full of regret? Would it affect our marriage? These were questions I hadn't really thought about before. I didn't like thinking about them now, either.

"That and because her husband was a cheating bastard who broke her heart," Clarissa recited.

"Oh, hey," I said, raising my hand. "We don't use that kind of language around here."

She looked confused. "Whatever. You sure have a lot of rules, you know?"

"We'll try to fill you in on the others as they come up."

She didn't look too happy at that prospect.

"At least Hallie has you now." I could hear the ziiinnng of the line going into the water as I fished away.

But she brightened. In fact, it was the happiest look I could remember seeing on her face. "Yeah! She's got me. She says that all the time. Thank God she's got me. Thank God she's got at least one person to love who loves her back."

That struck me speechless. What terrible thing to put on a little girl. Poor Clarissa. Heck, poor Hallie, if she really felt that way.

"You want something to drink?" I finally managed.

"Do you have anything good?"

"I bet I could rustle up some lemonade."

She shrugged again. "Whatever."

Not knowing what else to do, I flipped on the television and left her staring at it while I went into the kitchen. Unlike Erin, who would have followed me and asked questions, or else gone to pursue her own interests, Clarissa sat on the sofa where I'd found her, staring at the images on the box. And she continued to do the same thing once I'd brought her a glass of cold, tart lemonade.

I took two more glasses down to Erin's room. At least the door wasn't closed all the way this time, and I nudged it open with my foot. Erin and Zoe looked up from where they lay on their stomachs on the bed, a *Girls' Life* magazine open in front of them.

"I thought you were working on Zoe's organic gardening project," I said, handing each of them a sweating glass.

"We're done for now," Zoe said. She was a tall, athletic thing, prone to skinny jeans, T-shirts with obscure band names on them, and vintage high-top sneakers.

"You didn't kick Clarissa out, did you?"

They exchanged glances.

My heart sank. "You didn't."

Erin swung her feet to the floor. "No. But we didn't stop her from leaving, either. She's bossy, and she made fun of Zoe's project."

"She's weird," Zoe said.

"Mostly she's lonely," I said. "Give her another chance?"

Again the glance. They were like sisters in their silent communication. I got it. Meghan and I were like that, too. I was glad to see the newcomer hadn't broken that bond.

"Okay," Zoe said, which was fitting since she'd been the one Clarissa insulted.

"Thanks," I said. "She's in the living room watching television."

"Will she watch what we want?" Erin asked. Sure enough, ever since the ice cream incident she didn't seem as interested in Clarissa.

"I'm sure you guys can work that out," I said.

NINETEEN

I SNAGGED MEGHAN IN the front hallway as her client left. Pulling her into the kitchen, I quickly updated her on the girls.

"Darn it," she said. "I thought it would be okay for an hour if they were all together. Mrs. Patterson's sciatica has been acting up. I told Erin in no uncertain terms not to leave the house."

"Nah. It was fine," I said. "Listen, I'm sorry I bailed on you to go over to Daphne's. Still it's good I went. She was frantic about Nate." Not to mention Barr would have probably gone through her unmentionables if I hadn't been there.

"Poor girl. Any news on how he's doing?" she asked.

I shook my head. "Barr said he'd call if he heard anything. Listen, I know you have another client at three. Would it be okay with you if I made a quick run down to Bette's before then?"

Her eyebrows knotted. "What for?"

A grin sneaked onto my face. "I want to commission a mask for Barr's birthday. What do you think?"

She looked wry. "Would the mask be of you or of him?"

"Of... hmmm... no, I think it would be funnier if it were of him. They're great, don't you think? She seems to capture some kind of essence in each one." Okay, so I was pretty proud of myself for coming up with such a cool gift idea.

"They're unique, all right," Meghan said.

I paused. "Wouldn't you want one?"

A few moments as she thought about it. "Only as long as Bette caught something about myself that I *like*."

"Good point," I said. "I don't want Barr to think we're making fun of him. I'll take a couple different pictures and ask her advice."

"I'll hold down the fort," she said, reaching into the refrigerator and removing the half-empty pitcher of lemonade I'd made earlier.

As I walked down the street to Bette's I thought about what Clarissa had told me about her aunt. Hearsay at best, though I was inclined to believe it. Hallie wanted kids, couldn't have kids, had a cheating husband,and went through a bad divorce. If all that was true, was it enough to explain her behavior toward Nate? Or had he really done something to deserve it? Frankly, Nate didn't strike me as the type to incite passion. But what did I know?

I knew this: No matter what Nate had done, no one deserved the kind of fanaticism she showed. Possibly Hallie was a little unbalanced to begin with, and the divorce had sent her over the edge. If she really felt Clarissa was the only person she could love who would love her back, it might explain why she became so angry at the slightest rejection—from Nate or anyone else.

But was it enough to kill someone over?

Alexander greeted me at the sidewalk and accompanied me to Bette's front door, his thick tail swishing back and forth. The inner door was closed, and there was no answer to my knock. I should have called first. I'd just turned around to leave when the sound of the deadbolt turning stopped me. I stepped back to see her peering out of the screen.

"Sophie Mae!" Then she spied the photos in my hand. "Oh, no. Not again."

I looked down. "Oh! No, don't worry. These are of Barr."

"Barr?"

"I want to commission a mask. I got the idea when we were here yesterday."

She hesitated. "Well, then." Pushing the screen door open, she said, "You'd better come in and tell me what you want."

I entered the living room behind her. That metallic, subterranean smell greeted my entrance, and there seemed to be more clay spatter than ever—on the floor and on Bette herself. From the look of things, I'd interrupted work on some big project. A big table in the center of the room was covered with tools and buckets, and as I watched she tucked plastic sheeting around her work in progress.

"Coffee?" she asked.

"No, thanks." I scanned the masks on the walls. Handing her the pictures of Barr—one a candid shot of him laughing, and another from our wedding at his parents' Wyoming lodge—I moved closer to the display. "Are these all commissions?"

"No, I just liked the subjects. A couple are people I know; others are from photos I took. The Woodland Park Zoo is a great place to find willing subjects, especially kids."

Some of the clay faces were comical, others almost tragic. I was drawn to a laughing boy, an old woman with wise eyes, and a young woman looking toward the heavens. A little girl with a gap-toothed grin hung next to the face of a funny teddy bear. On the other side of her was a bearded man who looked fourteen kinds of weary.

But three masks in particular snagged my interest. Unlike the mild caricatures all the others represented, these were realistic to the nth degree. Two were of women, and one a man. One of the women was older, and you could practically see how her mouth would move if she talked, how her eyes would dance when she smiled. The others were younger, but again the whole was more than the sum of the parts. That wasn't clay on the wall. Those were the closest thing to actual people you could get with a static medium.

Even better than the funny, quirky representation of Barr that I had imagined.

"I want one like that." I pointed to the older lady. "Real looking. Can you do that from the wedding photo? I'd like to be able to see the way he looks at me in that one, even when he's not around." Never mind that this present was supposed to be for him, not me.

But Bette was shaking her head. "I'm sorry."

"Please?"

"I'm sorry. Honest. I know what it's like to want to be able to see the way someone looks at you, no matter what happens to them."

Oh. Gosh. I hadn't intended to sound so morbid. "I meant if he's at work or something."

"I can't do it from a photo."

Watching her, I saw a deep sadness descend. I couldn't help myself. "Who is that?" I asked, pointing to the older woman's face again.

"My mother. She died last year."

Well, now I felt lower than slug snot. "I'm sorry."

But Bette shook her head. "It's okay. I have that to remember her by. I did it before her face faded in my mind."

I knew exactly what she meant. I had a hard time bringing my first husband's face clearly to mind, and he'd only been dead for seven years. On the other hand, what if I had a realistic mask of his face on the wall? Or of Barr's should something happen to him? The thought of either made me inexplicably shudder.

"And the others?" I ventured.

She shrugged. "Friends. From when I was still experimenting, still deciding what my niche would be." But the sorrow about her mother lingered.

"Well, maybe Barr would prefer something with some humor," I said, trying to lighten the mood. "What do you think? Are you too busy to do it by the end of next month?"

"I'll manage it—for you." Her response warmed me. This was a woman who truly loved what she did. "How about I put together a few ideas from these photos using that software you saw me use yesterday, and you can pick which one you like best."

"Sounds great. Oh, speaking of that software—and yesterday—we found out who the first victim was."

"First victim?" Her smile dropped.

Of course. She didn't know about Nate.

"I found Nate Snow in the popcorn patch at the farm this morning. Someone hit him over the head, too."

Her hand moved to her throat.

"He's in the hospital now," I said.

"So he's not dead?"

"He's in a coma. We don't know much else. His girlfriend is with him now."

"I didn't even know he had a girlfriend."

"Daphne Sparks."

She nodded. "Oh, sure. Nice girl. Well, I hope he's all right." She made a tsking sound. "Why on earth would someone do such a thing?"

"We don't know yet, but I suspect it has something to do with wild jealousy." I saw the intrigued expression on her face, and barely stopped myself from spilling the beans. They were, after all, my theoretical beans, not official beans, and either way not ready for spilling. But I could tell her something. "At least Nate was able to tell me who the woman was that Meghan found in the compost."

Her eyebrows rose, and she leaned forward. "Really? Who?"

Yep, there's something about being instrumental in finding the truth that hooks you into the rest of a murder investigation all right.

"Her name was Darla Klick. She was an ornithologist, and it seems she specialized in birds of prey. Merlins, if Erin is right. Did you know her?"

Bette looked the "duh" at me.

"Oh. Right. You would have recognized the picture. You know, Jake Beagle seemed to remember her from a few years back, but couldn't place her. I'm glad Nate was able to let us know who she was. Us and her family. He popped up to Arlington to let her parents know before his encounter with the mysterious bludgeoner."

She shook her head. "What the heck is going on out at that farm? It makes me want to stay away."

"Oh, no. Don't do that. The Turners can't afford to lose volunteers in the middle of the harvest season. This year could make or break that farm. But," I held up my finger, "Barr suggested that we work in pairs, and we're already scheduled to work together tomorrow. So I'll pick you up in the morning. Unless you want to ride your bike?"

"No, I'll go with you," she said absently.

We both paused for a few moments, digesting all the weirdness.

Finally, I said, "I'd better get going. Her parents are nervous, so Clarissa Turner is staying with us until things get sorted out at the farm—and Meghan has a client arriving soon."

She nodded. "I'll let you know when I've got computer mock-ups of Barr's mask."

It took me less than three minutes to walk home, but by the time I got there I was worried all over again. What if Nate died, and never had a chance to tell us who hit him? And what about Daphne? How much danger was she really in?

TWENTY

I CALLED THE HOSPITAL when I got home, but they wouldn't give me any information about Nate because I wasn't family. They said I needed a code word, patient bill of rights, yada, yada, yada. Sheesh. It was a hospital, not a speakeasy.

Meghan was busy with her last massage client for the day, the girls had given up on the television and were back in Erin's room, and Barr wasn't home yet. Likely he wouldn't be much before dinner. When I tried calling him, he didn't answer.

We had a rule that if either of us was in the middle of something we didn't have to answer. Of course, that worked for him a lot more than it did for me, but I sure didn't want to mess up a stakeout or interrupt a suspect interview to ask my hubby to pick up some milk on the way home from work. And if we had a real emergency then we followed the first call with a second one right away.

This wasn't an emergency, not like that. I just wanted to know if Nate was still comatose. At least the hospital had confirmed that he'd been admitted to the ICU, so I knew he was still alive.

Still, being in the ICU wasn't a good sign. I looked at my watch. When Meghan's client left I'd have enough time to run to Everett and back before dinner. Maybe someone could tell me something if I was standing right in front of them. Plus, I could check on Daphne.

Pop music drifted down the hallway from Erin's room, prompting me to see how things were going with the prepubescent trio. My young housemate sat in her desk chair with a towel draped around her shoulders. I immediately thought of Cyan's purple locks and cast about the room for a telltale box of hair color. But her hair was dry, and as I watched, Clarissa fished a bobby pin out of a pile on the dresser. She tucked another of Erin's curls into the updo and stood back to inspect her work, nodding to herself.

I had to admit, it looked pretty cute. Perhaps Clarissa had a future in cosmetology. Heck, maybe she could do something with my unruly mop.

Zoe lolled on the bed looking bored as all get out, Brodie at her feet. Seeing me in the doorway, she gestured toward the other two with her chin and rolled her eyes. I grinned. That didn't appear to improve her disposition.

"You guys need anything?" I asked.

Murmurs in the negative assured me all was well for now, and I went downstairs to check in with Cyan and Kalie. They had finished labeling all those tiny lip balm tubes, a tedious task for young eyes that I'd learned to avoid. I asked them to pack up a small wholesale order while I made a dent in my growing pile of paperwork, and then I sent them home. A few minutes after four o'clock I shut down the computer and headed back upstairs.

The door to Meghan's office was open, and her client was gone. She stood next to the file cabinet, perusing a single sheet clipped into a file folder.

"Is that Darla Klick's file?"

She closed it and put it on the top of the file cabinet. "Yes." Terse.

"Anything interesting?"

"That's confidential, Sophie Mae."

I just looked at her.

It took about ten seconds to crack her. "I gave her two regular massages," she said. "I noted how tense and nervous she seemed to be."

"Which is probably why she sought you out anyway," I said. "Do you know how she heard of you?" Meghan didn't advertise per se. After seven years as a massage therapist in a town the size of Cadyville, regular clientele and word-of-mouth garnered plenty of business.

"I noted that, too. It was Dr. Beagle who recommended me."

"Huh. He did mention that he thought he'd seen her in a professional capacity when I showed him the photo Bette adjusted for us. But he couldn't remember her name."

Meghan's mouth pursed. "There was one other thing."

I waited.

"She told me she was in her first trimester. I always ask new female clients of child-bearing age if they're pregnant."

"Oh," I breathed, leaning my tush against her desk. "Oh, my. I wonder if Jake knew?"

"That really would be confidential, you know."

"Of course. And it was years ago. I wonder what happened to the child?"

"Didn't Sergeant Zahn talk to her parents? Did they say anything about a grandchild?"

"Not that I know of. I'll follow up with Barr tonight," I said. "Right now I'm going over to the hospital to get an update on Nate. The girls are in Erin's room."

"Zoe, too?"

"Last I looked."

"Do they look like clowns painted up to go to the circus?" She dropped the file back into the cabinet.

My eyes crinkled in a smile. "Not so much. But your daughter sure has a fancy hairdo now."

"Oh, God," Meghan groaned. "Clarissa didn't cut her hair, did she?"

"Nah. You'll like it. It's pretty."

"We'll see."

We went out to the entryway together.

"How 'bout CSA soup tonight?" my housemate asked.

"Sounds good to me."

One side of her mouth turned down. She paused. Licked her lips. "Um, about this morning."

"Isn't that supposed to go, 'About last night'?"

"Okay, both."

I held up my hand. "You know, I was going to quiz you pretty hard when I saw Kelly stumble into the kitchen after you this morning, but darlin' it's really none of my business. It's got to be hard enough living with another couple in the house without us asking you about your personal life. Besides, it's not like I'm a prude."

She snorted. "I don't have a personal life when it comes to you, Sophie Mae. Never have, and probably never will. Erin is the only reason I've been so careful about overnighters with Kelly. If it weren't for worrying what she'd think, I'd move that man into this house lock, stock, and parabolic microphone."

"Erin's got a pretty good head on her shoulders," I ventured.

"She does. But after all that mess with her father, his girlfriends, his crazy mother, and then him up and leaving the state altogether, I don't want to do anything that could potentially hurt her."

"Of course not." We'd been through a lot of growing pains with Erin. Her resilience was impressive. At one point she'd been quite jealous of Kelly; now she loved him to death. "Are you afraid you guys won't last?" I asked.

"Not at all. I'm pretty sure this is, you know, *it*. We've moved slowly—"

"I'll say."

"—and been pretty careful. We've talked about a lot of things to make sure we're on the same page."

"So why don't you guys get married?"

Meghan stepped around her desk. "For one thing, he hasn't asked me."

"But you've talked about it?"

"We did for a while."

I grimaced. "Did he act like a scared bunny?"

But she shook her head in the negative.

"Well, for heaven's sake, Megs!" I struggled to keep my voice low so the girls wouldn't hear. "Why don't you ask him?"

"Uh."

Putting my hands on her shoulders, I gently shook her. "Do it. Be a real family."

She stared at me with a slightly dazed expression. "Oh, my God. Of course. It's the only real solution."

I watched her wander out of her office toward the kitchen, no doubt already rehearsing in her mind. Good Lord. Meghan was one of the brightest bulbs I knew, but when it came to love she sometimes needed a seeing-eye dog.

Arf.

For once I didn't get lost trying to find the hospital parking garage in Everett. Of course, it hadn't been that long since I'd been there, and it was still daylight. But I did have to ask the nice gentleman at the information desk how to get to the ICU. An elevator ride and a few turns later, I spied Daphne sitting down the hall in a small lounge, her tall frame folded into a chunky, multi-colored chair. It wasn't until I veered toward her that I spied the two older women in the chairs next to her. I didn't know the one who wore the shapeless batik dress and sported thick gray dreadlocks. She held a cell phone to her ear with one hand and gesticulated with the other. But the woman sitting next to her was none other than Ruth Black, who had bullied Sergeant Zahn into letting her see Meghan's grisly find.

As I approached, Daphne looked up with a mixture of gratitude, relief, and weariness and lifted her hand in greeting.

Ruth rose and met me at the entrance of the lounge. "Hello, dear." She hugged me, smelling of cinnamon, rosewater, and hair gel. Her short white spikes glistened with it. Today she wore a pink, crocheted shell with a white cotton skirt and tennis shoes.

"Hello, yourself," I said. "You heard about Nate, then?"

"From your husband, actually."

"Really? When did you see Barr?"

A smile crinkled her crow's feet, and she leaned forward, searching my face.

"What?" I asked.

"I can't tell if you're glowing or not. I ran into your handsome man in the drugstore. He was buying one of those little kits. You know, the ones where you pee on a stick?"

I gaped at her.

Ruth patted my arm and whispered, "Don't worry. I haven't told anyone."

"Um, thank you," I managed.

Sheesh. Barr must be anxious indeed if he'd made that purchase himself. I reminded myself to take my temperature again when I got home.

"Anyway, your hubby told me about poor Nate and that Daphne was watching and waiting here, so I thought I'd stop by and check on her while Uncle Thaddeus is playing poker over at the Senior Center," Ruth said as we continued into the lounge.

"Hey." I sank onto the chair across from Daphne. "Any news? They wouldn't tell me anything on the phone."

She shook her head. "He's the same. The doctor says he's stable, but there's something funny in his eyes when he says it."

"There's some pressure on Nate's brain," Ruth explained. "It's quite worrisome." She picked up a bundle of knitting from the seat of the chair to Daphne's left and settled in, needles bobbing in and out of what appeared to be an elaborately patterned lace shawl.

I reached out and squeezed Daphne's arm. She nodded acknowledgment as the other woman ended her call. She shifted in her chair to look at me.

"This is Nate's mom, Faith Snow," Daphne said. "And this is Sophie Mae Ambrose."

"Ms. Snow." I nodded.

She stuck out her hand. "Call me Faith. Any friend of Nate's… well, you know. Sophie Mae… aren't you the one who found him?" She looked to Daphne for confirmation.

"I'm afraid so," I said.

"Well, I'm glad you did, because Nate might've died if you hadn't."

Not knowing what to say to that, I didn't say anything at all. But I'd already taken a liking to her. She seemed down-to-earth and practical. I wondered what she did for a living since the dream commune she and her friends started had been sold out to The Man.

"And Nate's dad . . . ?" I ventured.

"He's working on a fishing boat in Alaska. I just spoke with him. He'll be here tomorrow or the next day."

I licked my lips and tried to work out how to ask Faith about Darla Klick without coming across as an insensitive jerk. So far the information I'd gleaned about her was sketchy and even contradictory. Nate's best friend for years, a nice girl who loved birds. Or, according to Allie, a troubled, promiscuous teen with substance abuse problems. There was a story, if only I could get at it. Was muckraking like that really necessary, though? Would knowing Darla's story help find her killer?

Well, it wouldn't hurt.

"Um," I finally said. Brilliant.

Faith and Daphne both looked at me expectantly. Ruth cocked her head to one side, and her hands slowed.

I scooted my chair forward, keeping my attention on Faith. "I was wondering if you'd mind telling me a little more about Nate and Darla. He mentioned that you used to live in a commune?"

She smiled a sad smile. "It was such a great place—and a great way to raise kids. I still miss it. Nate told you it was on Camano Island?"

"Mmm, hmm."

Daphne turned in her seat, as did Ruth. Faith had our attention.

"We called it Happy Daze." She gave a little snort and held up her hand. "I know, I know. Pretty silly. But we were young and goofy. It started as three couples who went to school together at Western University up in Bellingham. We were all dreamers, I guess, and we felt like we'd been born a decade too late. Then, on a field trip, we visited a Hutterite settlement in eastern Washington. That was it. We wanted to live in a similar community, working together, being self-sufficient, but without the heavy religious overtones.

"Over the period of a few months, Nate's father and I found a few other people on campus who liked the idea. We'd sit around and drink wine and talk about how it would be. Shared work, huge gardens, centralized kitchen, spreading the load, interconnected and living like a huge, warm family. A one-room school house, a little chapel on the hill. Our imaginations created quite the idyllic scene. When we learned of a piece of land for lease, off grid, we set out to make it happen."

"Was it all you imagined?" Ruth asked. In her lap her knitting needles moved with lightening speed.

"Of course not. When you put people into any equation you get their weaknesses, too. There was conflict, certainly, and sometimes we had to ask people to leave. But there were central tenets we lived by, that we truly believed, and they created what structure we did have. Most people genuinely wanted to make it work, and God knows we were chock full of energy, if not wisdom. We made a lot of practical mistakes at first, simply because we didn't know what we were doing. But we asked for advice and read books and worked things out for ourselves. We learned so much in the first few years. Good thing, too, because otherwise we would have starved."

I couldn't help but raise my eyebrows at that.

"Well," Faith acquiesced. "Maybe we wouldn't have starved, but we would have had to give up our dream. In some ways that would have been worse."

Nate's mom was obviously still a dreamer. He had some of that quality, too. A kind of determined innocence.

She grimaced. "Yes, by the time it all came to an end the place ran very well. Not only could we support ourselves, but we made money from excess crops, from harvesting the ocean, and from some of the items we produced."

"Like what?"

"Well, we had goats by then, and sold the cheese we made. And we had llamas, and they produced lots of soft, fluffy—"

"Fiber!"

She looked surprised. "Right."

"Ruth taught me to spin last year," I explained with a nod to my fiber arts mentor. She glanced up from her knitting, obviously pleased.

"Sorry to interrupt," I said. The more Faith talked the more I had to agree with Daphne's assessment. The commune Nate had grown up in did sound pretty darn wonderful. Difficult, but if you weren't afraid of hard work, still wonderful.

"And that's where Nate and Darla first met? You see with both of them ... attacked ... I thought perhaps there was something about their relationship that sparked someone to, well, that caused ..." I trailed off, feeling lame and stupid and insensitive.

Faith nodded. "I'd be happy to share whatever I can if you think it would help. Daphne told me you help the police sometimes. What would you like to know?"

TWENTY-ONE

I GLANCED AT DAPHNE, then back at Faith. "Okay. How did Nate and Darla meet?"

"The Klicks were one of the original three couples. All our children were born after we started Happy Daze."

"Does Nate have siblings? Or Darla?"

"Nate has a brother who's one year older, and his sister is eight years younger. Darla had a younger sister as well—two years, I believe. She used to follow them around like a puppy. Made them crazy." Faith smiled, remembering.

My brother, Bobby Lee, had done that for a while when we were growing up. Now I'd give anything to have him around to bug me.

"So Nate and Darla were more or less raised together."

Faith nodded. "Their whole lives, until we had to disband. They became best friends in fourth grade."

“Did they ever … date?” I didn't even know if it were possible to date in a situation like that. “Or fall for each other, like romantically?”

I sensed more than saw Daphne stiffen in her chair.

“No,” Faith said, oblivious. A hint of regret shaded the word. “We all kind of hoped they would, and they might have eventually if—well, something happened that made that impossible.”

Daphne looked worried, her bottom lip clamped between her teeth. I remembered her reference the night before to a sad story. And Allie had said something about an accident.

Something flickered behind Faith's eyes, and she turned toward Daphne. “Did Nate tell you about it?”

The younger woman tipped her chin in the affirmative. “You mean the woman who fell out of the boat.”

“Right. Sophie Mae, do you know about that? It tore Nate and Darla apart.”

“Sounds pretty bad,” I said.

Ruth nodded her agreement, concern—and curiosity—all over her face.

Faith looked down at the floor and took a deep breath, as if bracing herself. The muscles in my neck and shoulders tightened in empathetic anticipation.

“There were a few people in our group of college friends who liked the whole idea of Happy Daze, but couldn't really commit to that lifestyle for any number of reasons. Most eventually lost touch, but one—Leigh Weber—visited us regularly over the years. She'd come help with harvest or when we raised a new building. Sometimes she'd bring a special friend to show the place off to.

Often she'd talk about making the leap, joining us full-time. But then that would fade in the face of her work or love life or whatever. We would have welcomed her with open arms."

Faith paused, staring unseeing at the generic watercolor painting on the opposite wall of the ICU lounge. I could almost see the past turning over in her mind. "It was late October, eleven, no, twelve years ago. For once a spate of dry weather had been forecast over the weekend, and it seemed the perfect time for our harvest party. The date always changed according to the weather and our workload, but sometime every fall we prepared an abundance of food, built a bonfire, and celebrated another year of successfully living from the land. It was half pagan, half Thanksgiving.

"Leigh always tried to make it out to the island for those parties, and though some years she wasn't able to, that year she did. She brought someone she'd been seeing for a while, and planned to stay for a week afterward to help us get ready for the coming winter. There was always so much to do that time of year—preserve the garden produce, erect cold frames, plant cold weather crops, lay in a supply of wood for heat, winterize our homes. And sure enough, right after they arrived Leigh began talking about staying forever." She pressed her lips together before continuing.

"Happy Daze was near the beach, and we harvested much of our food from Puget Sound. We dug clams and gathered oysters, fished for salmon, and set out a series of crab pots in regular locations."

"Nice," I said, thinking of how many people pay big bucks for such delicacies. But talk about local and easily accessible food in the Pacific Northwest.

Faith's smile didn't quite reach her eyes. "It was. And in the early days, we relied heavily on that bounty. But by that October we'd been living together on that land for almost twenty years, and we had our act together."

"How old was Nate?" I asked.

"Seventeen, almost eighteen. He wanted to take a year to wander, and then planned to go to Western and study agriculture. He's always had a green thumb."

"You didn't mind him leaving?"

"As Kahlil Gibran says, you don't own your children. His father and I agreed that taking a year or so to explore the world would be good for him. It would be his choice whether to come back to us or not."

I wondered whether I'd be such a level-headed parent. I liked to think I would. Of course, I liked to think a lot of things.

"So that October Nate and Darla—she was a year younger—went out to pull the pots so we'd have plenty of Dungeness crab to boil up for the party that night. Leigh offered to go with them."

The woman who fell out of the boat. Oh, dear. I exchanged glances with Daphne.

"That wasn't unusual—she'd gone out several other times. So the three of them went down, launched our little boat, and headed out."

"Little boat," I repeated before I could stop myself.

Faith grimaced. "Not that little. It was a sixteen-foot, aluminum fishing boat, which was perhaps a bit small to take out on the Sound. But the water was calm in our little inlet, and the crab pots were relatively close to shore. At least most of them were. The kids had gone out loads of times, and we never worried about them. What we had never known was that Leigh couldn't swim."

I winced. "No life jackets?"

"Two, actually, in the boat at all times. Usually only two people at a time went out, you see."

"And Nate and Darla could both swim?"

"Oh, yes. We made sure of that."

Still. Puget Sound wasn't some tropical paradise. The beaches were rocky, and the average water temperature was less than fifty degrees.

"Everyone was so busy and excited about the party that night. No one even realized there were only two life vests and three people. And of course, Leigh, being a responsible adult, insisted that the kids wear them. Nate swears he never would have let her go out there without one if he'd known she couldn't swim."

"She fell overboard," I said.

Faith closed her eyes. "Reaching for the buoy above a crab pot. The water wasn't choppy when they went out, but a wind had come up as they worked. Even then the waves aren't what most people would even call waves, but a little one rocked the boat at exactly the wrong time and she flipped into the water." She was talking faster now. "Nate reached for her, but she was panicking. He realized she couldn't swim, and the boat was drifting away from her. He dove in to save her." Her gaze latched onto the glass door that led down the sterile hallway to the ICU, where her unconscious son lay.

I watched her anguish in silence. This story didn't end well for Leigh. I already knew that. But now coupled with her comatose son, I wondered at Faith's ability to tell it.

"He couldn't, though. Save her. By the time he got to her, she had already drowned. By the time they got back Nate was almost delusional from hypothermia. He'd been in the water for almost ten minutes, Darla said. I was so grateful she'd stayed in the boat and could bring them both back. Otherwise, we might have lost all three." She blinked back tears. "That was the end of our harvest festivals. A couple years later we lost the whole place."

Daphne slid her arm around Faith's shoulder, and the older woman closed her eyes and leaned her cheek against the younger woman's shoulder. Her breath was ragged as she struggled to regain control of her emotions.

She was one tough lady.

After a minute she sat up and met my eyes. Hers were red, but dry. Daphne kept her hand on her arm.

"Thank you for telling me," I said. "I know it was difficult, and I don't have any idea how it could have any bearing on the attacks at the Turner farm, but it does tell me a lot about Nate and Darla's relationship that they went through that together."

"Nothing was ever the same for those two after that," Faith said. "The guilt about drove Nate crazy. He left to wander as he planned, but he never did go to college. He got involved with drugs for a while, and never settled down for more than a few months until he ran into Tom Turner."

"They knew each other from Happy Daze, right?"

Faith nodded. "Tom and Allie joined us late. Both of them understood farming, and they fit right in. That little girl of theirs was a sweetie, too. I can't remember her name."

"Clarissa," I said.

"Right. Thank God Tom offered Nate a job. Ever since he's been at the Turners' farm there in Cadyville, Nate has been on track." She patted Daphne's hand on her arm. "This girl has been a good influence, too."

Daphne smiled.

"Did Nate ever mention Allie's sister, Hallie?" I asked.

Puzzled expressions from both Faith and Ruth greeted my question.

Ruth frowned. "Why on earth would he?"

Daphne said, "It doesn't really matter, does it, Sophie Mae?"

Right. Maybe better not to bring that up right now.

I returned to my original line of questioning. "What about Darla? Allie mentioned something about an incident that involved Tom."

"Oh, that was just a big misunderstanding," Faith said. "And Allie overreacted. Darla had emotional issues after the accident. Anxiety and severe depression. The Klicks sent her to rehab once, and it helped for a while. When she came back she avoided Nate. It got so each reminded the other of what had happened. After the commune broke up they lost touch, on purpose, I think." She sighed. "If only they could have talked to each other about it instead."

"I think they did," Daphne said. "Nate said he and Darla had a really good discussion about the accident and how it had affected their lives before, well, you know."

Before she was killed.

How could I ever have thought she'd be jealous of Nate's old friend? Nate had told her about Leigh drowning right before his eyes—maybe even in his arms. So Daphne knew she didn't have anything to worry about.

But Hallie didn't know the nature of the bond between Nate and Darla. Hallie only thought in terms of ... what did she think in terms of? Clarissa's comment came back to me.

Thank God she's got at least one person to love who loves her back.

I couldn't quite figure out Hallie. Was she the evil twin, or was she just lost and kind of pathetic?

A glance at the clock on the wall reminded me of the time. I stood. "It was nice to meet you, Faith. Thank you for talking with me. We're all sending Nate our thoughts and prayers."

"Thank you." She stood and gave me a hug.

"Daphne, can I get your cell number?" I was worried about her and wanted to be able to check in on her—and on Nate.

She tore off a corner of a magazine on the table and scribbled it down. As she handed it to me, I remembered another question.

"Faith? Do you know anything about Darla's child?"

Still another layer of sadness crossed her features. "I know she was pregnant, but she never had the baby. She lost it early on."

Speechless, I struggled not to react. My mouth was so dry I couldn't swallow. Could hardly breathe.

Ruth made a noise of sympathy and paused in her knitting. She looked up at me, eyes full of understanding, and then she gave a single, slow shake of her head. Don't go there, Sophie Mae, it said. There's enough to worry about without adding that to the mix.

I blinked and returned a slight nod.

Faith didn't notice any of it. "Her boyfriend at the time lived in Cadyville. After the miscarriage, Darla left him. But her mother told me losing the baby triggered a turnaround for Darla. It could have so easily gone the other way, you know? But something about that time convinced her that life was too short to be unhappy all the time. She got her degree, lost a bunch of weight, and started reconnecting with old friends." Faith tried a smile. "So perhaps it wasn't all bad, you know?"

"Maybe you're right," I said.

But as I drove out of the parking lot, I had to wonder whether reconnecting with old friends was why Darla Klick had been killed.

TWENTY-TWO

THE COMPLEX SMELL OF vegetables cooking together wafted through the open front door, through the yard, and all the way to the sidewalk out front. Inside, the murmur of voices drew me into the kitchen. Erin and Zoe stood on opposite sides of the butcher block table, each with a cutting board and small knife. The wet paper towels Meghan had placed under the boards so they wouldn't slip on the smooth table surface peeped out from the edges. Erin quickly sliced kale into ribbons and reached for a red bell pepper. Her hair was still piled high on her head as if she were going to a prom, an amusing juxtaposition with her denim shorts and purple-striped T-shirt. Zoe hacked at a zucchini. Clarissa sat at the end, chin resting on one palm, looking bored. Meghan turned from the pot she was stirring on the stove, and one look told me things were still tense with the girls.

"Whatever you've got stewing up in that pot is going to make the whole neighborhood hungry," I said.

"I know," Erin said. "When Mom said we'd make veggie soup with all the good stuff you brought home yesterday, I thought it would be kind of boring."

"It is boring," Clarissa grumped.

"Is not. It smells good and it's going to taste even better. Mom made bread, and we've even got homemade butter and jam to put on it."

I tried to keep from smiling. Erin wasn't usually such an advocate for the from-scratch and local cooking Meghan and I tended toward, occasionally grumbling at the lack of mac-and-cheese from a box and day-glo orange snack crackers. Clarissa's dismissive attitude had apparently sparked her defense mechanism.

Zoe doggedly whacked away, ignoring them both.

"So are we going vegetarian tonight?" I asked Meghan.

"I thought we could add some Italian sausage, pasta, and beans, and make this into a minestrone."

Yum. "Kelly will be here?"

She blinked, and a small smile turned up one corner of her mouth. "Yes." Our eyes met, and I saw her anticipation. It was going to be an interesting evening for those two.

"You all want to go out to a movie tonight?" I asked the girls. Meghan and Erin had been standing right there beside me when Barr asked me to marry him. Of course, they also knew it was coming, since he'd already worked out the idea of buying into Meghan's house and renovating it so I wouldn't have to leave what I thought of as my family. However, my friend might want a bit more privacy for what she was about to spring on her beau, and her look of happy relief at my suggestion confirmed it.

Erin stopped and looked at me with suspicion. "Why?"

"I thought you liked to go to the theater," I countered.

"Well, I can't go," Zoe said. "I've got a riding lesson tonight."

Clarissa sniffed.

"How 'bout you?" I asked. "Do you like movies?"

"I guess. But nothing animated. Cartoons are for little kids."

"I'm sure we can find something appropriate."

"Hallie takes me to R-rated movies."

"Well, that won't be happening tonight." Get used to it, kid.

Something croaked in Zoe's pocket, and we all turned to stare. She grinned and pulled out her phone. It made another frog noise.

"Mom just texted me," she said. "I gotta go."

As she followed her friend to the door, Erin threw a look at her mother. It said everyone on the whole planet had a cell phone except for Erin Bly and that totally sucked. Amazing, really what a single look from that kid could say.

Meghan sighed.

I sliced the sausage into the tomato-based soup burbling slowly on the stovetop, grabbed an apple, and headed down to my workroom. I hadn't eaten lunch, and any more time in that kitchen would see me ladling some of that fragrant soup into a bowl to "test."

A really big bowl.

On the work island Cyan and Kalie had left neat rows of foot scrub packaged into jars with Winding Road labels. The fresh scent of mint still curled through the air. I moved the jars to the storeroom shelves next to baskets of lip balm. The lavender-basil soap I'd poured two days before had solidified enough to cut. Heavy footsteps upstairs alerted me that Kelly had arrived. As I sliced and trimmed and carefully stacked the bars to cure in the storeroom, I wondered how Meghan would pop the question. Would she come right out and ask him to marry her? Or start with a "we have to talk" style discussion that would end in a proposal?

But even the potential of adding another member to the household couldn't keep my attention from wandering to the story Faith Snow had told me that afternoon. How quickly a life—or two—could be changed. Or ended. Most of the time we wander through our days assuming tomorrow will be very much like today, and that's usually a safe belief to hold because that's exactly what happens. But one event, one turning point, and everything is different. The awareness felt heavy while at the same time it made me feel fragile as glass.

Tentative.

Life was risky. Putting a child into the mix really upped the ante, too. I'd often smiled at Meghan's protective attitude toward Erin, but I understood it. If I had a baby, I'd more than understand it. I'd live it every day.

Was that why Meghan was so against my "little investigations"? Could I really keep involving myself in Barr's work if I had a child? How could Kelly possibly know enough about it to tell me I could?

I gathered the last of the soap trimmings to mash together for our own use—functional if not as pretty—when Clarissa yelled upstairs, followed by a sharp bark from Brodie. It sounded like a happy shout, though, and I took my time padding up to see what had caused Miss Grumpy Boots such joy.

No one was in the kitchen. Meghan's words drifted in from the entryway. "I'm sorry, but I can't do that. Allie and Tom want her to stay here tonight."

I rounded the corner and came up short. Hallie stood just inside the doorway. Looking past her, I saw the whippy red car parked at an angle to the curb, the driver's door hanging open. Meghan stood with her arms crossed over her chest, jaw set. Behind her, Kelly kept his hand on Clarissa's shoulder, despite how she leaned away from him. Erin looked on from the sidelines with wide eyes.

"What's going on here?" I moved to Meghan's side.

Hallie was a mess. Her jeans were tucked sloppily into knee-high riding boots that had never seen a stable. Her sleeveless blouse was rumpled, and a black satin bra strap had slipped down her arm. Her hair stuck out like she'd combed it with a piece of buttered toast, and her mascara was as smeared as if Erin had applied it. She peered at me with bleary eyes before an elaborate sneer distorted her features.

"You. You show up everywhere, don't you? Interfering, stirring things up. Nosy, nosy, nosy." The distinct smell of tequila drifted out on her words.

Oh, dear. I glanced at the clock. Not even six o'clock.

"It's your fault he got hurt. Your *fault*."

"Are you talking about Nate?" I asked.

"Of course I'm talking about Nate!"

"Hallie," I said with slow care. "Do you know what happened to Nate?"

She blew a very unladylike raspberry. "You think I'm stupid? Of course I do."

"Do you think that perhaps you ought to tell the police?"

A wily look flickered across her face. "Tell them what? Somebody hit him on the head. *They* told *me* that."

Was her innocence forced, or was this simply booze-induced stupidity? I tried again. "But you don't know who hit him?"

Her shoulders raised all the way to her ears and then dropped. She wove slightly back and forth in her boots. "How would I?"

Beside me, Meghan swallowed. I glanced back at Clarissa. Kelly had both of his hands on her shoulders, but she wasn't trying to pull away now. All her attention was on her aunt.

"C'mon, Clary. Go get your stuff. Let's go home."

"He won't let me." Clarissa's words held tears. I could tell Kelly was upset at having to restrain her, but no way would any of us let her leave with Hallie.

"Let her go!" Hallie took a step forward.

Meghan and I crowded together, blocking her way. "I'm sorry," I said. "Tom and Allie asked us to watch her, and that's what we're going to do. Maybe you could give me your car keys, and I'll call your sister to come pick you up."

She slowly shook her head. "I don't need anyone to come get me. I jus' miss my little Clary, is all. I want her to come back home. Miss her . . ."

"I'm sure she misses you, too," Meghan said.

"Do you, honey?" Hallie peered at her niece.

Clarissa gave a little nod, but frankly looked terrified. I could have killed her aunt right then and there.

"But she's spending the night with Erin," Meghan continued. "I think Sophie Mae had a good idea. I'm going to call Allie now."

"No!" Hallie held up her hands. "Don't bother her. It's okay. I'm going."

"Please wait. Come into the kitchen." Meghan reached for her. "I'll get you a cup of coffee and you can hang out with us for a while." She glanced over at me, and I nodded. Neither of us wanted Hallie around Clarissa in her current state, but what choice did we have?

But Hallie turned and pushed the screen door open, stumbling out to the porch and then, getting her bearings, ran down the steps.

"No, wait!" I followed her out the door, hoping against hope that she'd left the keys in the ignition. If I could get there first—

In the middle of the yard she stopped right in front of me, hunching over. I veered left to miss her, but she stood, fast, ramming her shoulder into my hip. Off balance, I went down with a loud *oomph*. Gasping, I came up on my knees, but she'd already made it to the car. Kelly flew past me and banged through the garden gate as Hallie slid into the car and slammed the door.

We all heard the automatic door locks.

Clarissa ran out into the yard. "Hallie! Wait, Hallie," she called.

But now her aunt was more interested in making a getaway than in her niece.

The Camaro's engine roared to life. Kelly jumped back as the vehicle accelerated backwards, then took off down the street with a squeal of tires on pavement. Watching it go, I saw Bette standing in her front yard with Alexander, head craned to see what the heck was going on at the Ambrose-Bly household.

How embarrassing.

"Are you all right?" Meghan asked, kneeling beside me.

"I'm fine," I wheezed, still on all fours. "Clarissa, honey? You okay?"

She shot me a fierce look—which promptly dissolved into tears.

TWENTY-THREE

Kelly went to call Barr while Meghan comforted Erin and I did my best to comfort Clarissa.

"What's wrong with her?" she sobbed into my shoulder. We were on the sofa, while Meghan and Erin had gone to Erin's room.

At least that implied Clarissa wasn't used to that kind of behavior from her aunt. I rocked her a little and murmured, "She's just upset. It'll be okay."

But would it? I still couldn't figure Hallie out. Was she drinking and carrying on because Nate got hurt? Because she hurt him? Did she have any idea how fine the line between love and hate was that she was straddling?

Was there something I didn't know?

Well, obviously, there was.

"How 'bout we call your mom," I said, almost sure Clarissa would reject the idea.

But she surprised me by nodding vigorously. In many ways she seemed years younger than Erin, in spite of her desire to grow up far too quickly.

"Okay. Wait here and I'll get the phone."

"I have mine," she said, reaching in her pocket.

"Let's use ours," I said. "I'd like to talk to your mom first, anyway." As I went into the front hall to retrieve the handset from its cradle, Barr's old white Camry pulled up in front. His car, not the department's. That meant he wasn't just stopping by the house on his way someplace else.

Good.

He ran up the walk. I met him at the door and gave him a quick kiss. "Be with you in a sec."

"Where's Kelly?" he asked.

"I think he went out back. Said something about checking the window locks."

Barr nodded and went to find him. I dialed the phone and waited, debating how to tell Allie about her sister.

"Sophie Mae? Is Clarissa okay?" God bless Caller ID.

"Hi, Allie. She's fine. Well, mostly fine."

"What's wrong?" Anxiety threaded her voice.

"Hallie stopped by to see her."

"Oh. I probably should have warned you. She was pretty upset when Tom told her we'd decided Clarissa should spend some time with Erin until the ... situation ... is resolved."

Situation, indeed.

"Did you know she'd been drinking?"

"What? No, of course not."

"We tried to get her to stay so we could call you, but she took off. I'm concerned that she's on the road." Not to mention how she handled that sporty car of hers even when sober.

"Oh, God. I'll call her—no, wait. What if she answers and she's driving and then she gets in a wreck? Should I wait?"

"Er, I don't know. We told Barr, so the police—and likely the sheriff's department—are on the lookout for her."

Allie was silent.

"I'm sorry," I said. "But she was acting pretty irrationally."

She sighed. "I suppose there are worse things than the police picking her up."

"I called to let you know what was going on, but also because Clarissa wants to talk to you. I think it kind of scared her to see her aunt like that, and she was trying to get Clarissa to come back home with her."

"Darn Hallie." For the first time Allie sounded truly angry at her sister. "We've put up with so much from her over the last year, and I keep making allowances and hoping she'd get over that crappy divorce. But her mood swings are getting more and more dramatic. She's getting worse, not better. Let me talk to my daughter."

Yes, ma'am. But I didn't take offense at her abrupt tone, because I knew it wasn't directed at me. Plus, I couldn't blame her.

"Hang on." I walked back into the living room and held the phone out to Clarissa, still huddled in the corner of the sofa. "Your mom's on the phone. Do you want me to leave you alone to talk to her?"

"Yes, please." It was the first polite thing she'd said to me.

I handed her the phone and went into the kitchen to add pasta shells to the minestrone. Barr and Kelly tromped up the stairs from my workroom as I stirred. My husband tucked his phone into his pocket as they entered the room. My gut twisted when I saw his face. Kelly didn't look very happy, either.

"What's wrong now?" I asked.

"That was Zahn. At least we know where Hallie was five minutes ago."

I rubbed my eyes. "Where?"

"The hospital."

My hand went to my throat. "Oh, no. What did she do?" I had visions of her breaking into the ICU and finishing the job on Nate.

"Found Daphne and Nate's mother and made another big scene."

I let out my breath. She hadn't gotten to Nate or hurt anyone. Still. "Darn it. The last thing Faith and Daphne need is some crazy woman making things even harder."

"Faith?" Barr asked.

Giving the soup on the stove another quick stir, I said, "Mrs. Snow. I went to the hospital this afternoon since they wouldn't give me any information over the phone. Now I have Daphne's number, so I can call her directly. I keep hoping Nate will wake up and *tell us who hit him.*" I couldn't keep the frustration out of my voice. There were too many possible suspects but no good ones except the one who had knocked me down in my own front yard and made a scene at the hospital.

"Unless you can get Hallie to confess," I said to Barr.

"That's unlikely, at least for now." His tone was wry.

"She is in custody, isn't she?" I asked.

Kelly snorted.

My shoulders slumped. "The hospital just let her go?"

"Not exactly," Barr said. "Once things escalated to the point where the floor nurse noticed what was going on, he called security. Apparently Hallie started yelling at Daphne, who turned around and yelled back. They were inches from a cat fight outside the ICU."

"Oh, God," I groaned. At least Daphne could stand up for herself.

"But it took security a couple minutes to get there," Barr said. "She scooted out before they arrived."

I slumped into a chair. "So she's still out there."

"Cadyville patrol is looking for her, and Everett, Monroe, and the county are on alert as well. We'll find her."

"Kelly told you she'd been drinking?"

Barr frowned. "Drinking or drunk?"

"Well ..." I hedged. "She seemed pretty loopy, but then again she seemed loopy when Daphne and I ran into her coming out of Nate's trailer, too. I could definitely smell tequila, though."

"Let's just hope she doesn't get into a wreck or hurt someone else."

Someone else?

"Do you think she's the one who attacked Nate?" Kelly asked before I could.

"Hard telling at this point." Barr refused to speculate without proper evidence. "I meant that if she's driving around drunk her car is a weapon that could hurt anyone who gets in her way."

Heck, the way she drove, her car was always a weapon.

"I'm going to check on Clarissa," I said.

Meghan and Erin came out of Erin's bedroom. Meghan looked as serious as a heart attack, but her grinning daughter had obviously recovered from Hallie's visit with the typical resilience of youth. So I was a little surprised when she ran up and gave me a big hug.

"Does it hurt?" Erin asked, patting my hip where Hallie had hit me.

"Sophie Mae?" Alarm echoed in Meghan's voice.

I squeezed Erin and waved with my free hand as if dispelling a fog. "That side's fine." My other hip, where I'd landed on the ground, would sport a fine bruise.

My housemates still looked concerned. So I pasted a big smile on my face and pushed Erin toward the kitchen. "Any chance I could get you to set the table?"

"Uh, sure," she said, taking a few steps.

Meghan gave me a hard look and then followed behind her.

In the living room, Clarissa was still on the phone. "But Mom, you have to let me come home. Hallie needs me ... I'll be careful, I promise ... please ...?" She looked at me with pleading eyes.

But I could tell Allie wasn't giving in. I couldn't blame her.

I gestured at Clarissa and whispered. "Let me talk to your mom before you hang up, 'K?"

She nodded. "Sophie Mae wants to talk to you again ... yeah ... okay ... I miss you, too." But not as much as she missed Hallie was my guess.

Offering an encouraging smile, I took the phone from her hand, crossed to the entryway and went into Meghan's office. I closed the door behind me. Clarissa didn't need to know what I was about to tell her mother.

"Allie? I have an update on Hallie."

She'd been angry at her sister before, but my news about the hospital and all the cops in the entire county being on the lookout for her doubled her fury. She agreed to call when Hallie came home.

If she came home.

"I don't think that's a good idea tonight," Barr said when I mentioned my idea of going to Monroe for a movie with the girls.

I hadn't had a chance to tell him why I wanted to give Meghan some alone time with Kelly. But he was right—with Hallie on the loose it would be better to hunker down at home. Together.

Meghan shrugged at me. "We'll watch something here, maybe play some board games."

Clarissa weighed in. "Board games are boring. That's why they call them bored games." She smiled at her joke, and after a moment so did Erin. "Don't you have video games?"

"On my computer," Erin said.

"Don't you have a game system for the TV? Or a Wii?"

Erin shook her head, ashamed at how lame our entertainment options were. She'd never minded before, preferring to read or engage in real-life activities.

"Ugh! How can you stand it?" Clarissa's lip curled in derision.

Erin shrugged. "I dunno. Do you have all that?"

Clarissa's chin rose. "Of course I do."

I tried to imagine Tom spending hard-earned money on such things when the budget was so tight their first year on the farm.

"Hallie gets me all kinds of stuff."

Ah. Of course. She'd probably made out quite well in the divorce.

"We could play poker," Erin said. "My Nana Tootie taught me how."

Clarissa sneered.

The evening did not get any easier after that. According to our guest, the soup had too many vegetables, bread and butter would make you fat, and fizzy cola products were vastly superior to homemade lemonade. She deemed the kale chips just plain weird and wanted chocolate ice cream for dessert when we only had vanilla. She didn't care for any of our suggestions for things to do after dinner. Eventually Erin gave up and went to her room, ostensibly to work on her novel. Even that met with disapproval from Clarissa.

At least Erin had gotten over feeling like we needed a houseful of video games, since Clarissa's credibility diminished with every complaint. The rest of us ended up sitting in the living room watching Clarissa channel surf until finally Meghan couldn't stand it any longer.

"Time for bed." She stood.

Kelly, Barr, and I followed suit.

Clarissa craned her head to look up at us. "But I want to stay up. Mom lets me stay up, you know."

"I highly doubt that," I said, remembering what Barr had said about waking up the family when he went to show them Darla's autopsy photo. Of course, just because he woke up the parents didn't mean their daughter wasn't playing some shoot 'em up in her room. "You and Erin can hang out in her bedroom."

Meghan fired a look at me, and I tried not to look sheepish.

"Whatever." Clarissa got off the sofa and trudged toward the hallway.

"Lights out in half an hour," Meghan called.

I ducked my head. "Sorry. I know Erin's had it with all the whining. But that little girl has some problems, not the least of which is her aunt. It's been a pretty tough day for her."

Barr put his arm around me. "You're right. She's not on her best behavior, but it's not exactly her fault."

To my surprise, Meghan rolled her eyes. "True, but it's not like she's ever on her best behavior."

My friend had had a pretty tough day, too.

TWENTY-FOUR

98.1°. Again.

Peering at the thermometer in the light over the bathroom sink, I couldn't see anything wrong with it. Maybe I hadn't been the best about keeping track of my temperature, but this was ridiculous. There ought to be at least some kind of blip in my chart.

But no. 98.1° had been the reading every single time.

I plugged the sink and ran hot water into it. Plunged the thermometer in. Waited.

Yep. 98.1°. The stupid thing was broken.

Into the garbage it went. Disgusted, I applied arnica salve to the bruise beginning to develop on my hip and pulled on a pair of soft, boy-cut shorts and a sexy little tank. Barr was in bed already, working on his laptop and trying to make a dent in departmental paperwork. I'd filled him in on what Faith Snow had told me about Nate and Darla's past. He'd dutifully jotted notes, but I could tell he didn't think there was any connection to the present. Frankly, I couldn't think of one, either.

Now I was tired as all get out. Still, I was willing to give the whole baby-making thing one more try.

Because tired or not, it was a lot of fun.

I swallowed my chasteberry supplement, mindful of the irony of the name since I'd read that it was supposed to promote fertility. I brushed my teeth and combed out my mop of hair, pretending the few white ones creeping in were just really, really blonde. On the way to the bedroom I stopped by the sitting room for a quick look at the calendar.

And stopped short.

I was usually as regular as regular could be on the monthly cycle front, but those dates weren't lying. In the flurry of activity and worry and, well, murder, I'd somehow missed the fact that I was late. Three days late.

How could that be? Not the being late—that made sense if I was pregnant, of course. But how could I not have cottoned on before? Maybe it had something to do with the mix of emotions racing through my mind at facing the idea of actually being with child. Racing through my mind, my heart, and my solar plexus.

Which might account for the heartburn.

I shuffled into the bedroom and crawled into bed, quiet as a mouse. Slid down until the covers reached my chin.

Distracted, Barr glanced down at me, then did a double-take. "What's wrong?"

Should I tell him? Well, why not?

"I'm late."

A grin pulled one side of his mouth up. "I wondered when you'd notice."

My eyes widened. "What do you mean? Since when do you keep track?"

"Since it became important. It's right there on the calendar."

I wiggled into an upright position. "Ruth told me she saw you buying a pregnancy kit in the drugstore."

"Did she, now? Ms. Black should pay more attention to her own purchases."

"Where is it?"

"Under the sink in the bathroom. Are you okay? This isn't exactly the reaction I expected."

I groped for the words. "For the first time this whole having-a-baby thing feels awfully … real."

"Awfully?" His smile held confusion.

"No, no. That didn't come out right. It's kind of scary, is all. Scary and wonderful and exciting and … can you understand?" I asked, not adding *terrifying* to the list. What was wrong with me? I was supposed to swoon and giggle at the thought that I might be preggers. And truth be told, I wanted to do those things, too. So many feelings swirling around made it hard to even breathe.

"Of course," he said, pulling me toward him.

But I pushed away and climbed out of bed. "I'll be right back."

He closed his laptop and put it on the bedside stand. "Okay. I'll be waiting."

I shuffled down the hallway, feeling more cold than sexy in my skimpy night gear and ducky slippers. The test sat in the back corner under the sink, right where Barr said it would be. Taking it out, I sank down on the closed toilet lid and read the directions.

It was the first time I'd taken a pregnancy test in my thirty-eight years. How had I managed that? My hands were actually shaking.

I opened the box and removed one of the wands. So you usually needed more than one? Was that the deal? It looked simple enough.

I did the deed.

And waited.

I filed my fingernails and applied cuticle cream, then rubbed cocoa butter on my elbows, knees, and heels. Barr sat in the other room. What kind of a wife was I? I should have been in there, waiting for the test results with him, but for some reason I wanted to know first. By the time the medicine cabinet was cleaned and neatly arranged the requisite amount of time had passed.

Much like I'd examined Darla's autopsy photograph, I flipped over the test and made myself look.

Barr sat exactly in the same position he'd been in when I'd gone into the bathroom. Now as I stood in the doorway, the tenderness in his gaze almost undid me.

I shook my head once.

He held out his arms. "Come here."

He turned the light off, and I put my head on his shoulder. He stroked my hair. "Take it one day at a time, Sophie Mae. We both will."

I nodded. "You're right, of course."

Soon his breathing became heavy and deep, and I felt him slip into slumber.

I tried to sleep, I really did. Disappointment and relief about not being pregnant warred. How was I supposed to feel? How did normal people feel in circumstances like that? Why did I always have to complicate things?

Counting backwards from one thousand didn't even dent my insomnia. And every time I tried to imagine myself drowsing on a warm, sandy beach, it reminded me of Faith Snow's story about the woman who drowned right in front of Nate and Darla. A tragedy that had followed them for the rest of their lives.

Still, Darla had turned her life around, getting her master's degree and following a passion for birds of prey. And it seemed Nate had found his footing on the Turner farm. I was sure that Faith was right about Daphne being good for him, too. I couldn't bear the thought that he might not ever come out of his coma, not when his life was finally on track. Not to mention that he was the only one who could confirm who had hit him over the head and killed Darla. Assuming, of course, that it was the same person.

See? There I went, complicating things again. Stick with the idea of one killer, Sophie Mae. At least until there was evidence to the contrary.

Was that killer Hallie? She fit the bill so well. Darla's time of death had been hard to pinpoint, so alibis were hard to come by for anyone associated with the farm—or the CSA. But did I really buy that Hallie was motivated by some kind of insane jealousy? Sure, she seemed unstable, but you'd have to be out-and-out crazy to kill someone you only suspect is an old flame of someone you used to date. And then to try and kill the old flame himself. Still…

I shook Barr awake.

"Wha…?"

"Don't you think you should put a guard on Nate's room?"

He sighed. "Dawson's been there since early evening. She's watching Daphne, too, since she refuses to leave the hospital."

"Oh. Okay. Good."

"Now go to sleep, Sophie Mae," he grumbled.

"Right. Goodnight."

"Mmmph."

Amazing, really, how quickly he could fall back into unconsciousness.

The other thing that struck me as odd was the way Darla had been buried in the compost. Whether the killer had known she was still alive or not, they still had to do the heavy lifting of shoveling the compost over her. I imagined they would have had to place her body at the edge of the pile and then climb at least partway up it to dislodge enough compost to bury her. That would have been very dirty work.

As Clarissa had said, Hallie didn't like to get dirty. Still, Mother Necessity made for some unusual choices.

Thoughts still swirling, I slid out from under the covers, slipped my ducky slippers back on and dug one of Barr's old sweatshirts out of the closet. Slipping it over my head, I padded down to the kitchenette. My favorite sleep-aid was a tea made of valerian root. It smelled horrible and tasted like sour dirt, but did the trick. I reached for the jar then saw it was empty. Some herbs were to be avoided during pregnancy—was valerian one of them? And what about my favorite single malt Scotch? Right out the window it would go once I was "with child."

Of course, the upside would be the child. And the thought of a little person who was part Barr and part me, was indescribably appealing. What was I so worried about?

I found some chamomile tea in the main kitchen downstairs, and put on the kettle by the low light over the stove. The house was still and dark, everyone in bed—Kelly, too, I assumed. Meghan might not have had the perfect evening to pop the question, but it was obvious she'd made a decision to bring him into the household day *and* night. Outside, the wind wuthered around the eaves and whispered through branches. I dodged furniture in the dark living room and, reaching the window, pulled back the curtain. Tree leaves danced against the moon-bright clouds above, but to the west the sky roiled dark and foreboding.

Back in the kitchen I brewed the tea, and with the soothing scent of chamomile steaming out of the mug, went downstairs to my workroom and turned on the small floor lamp in the corner by the big freezer. My selection of aromatherapy and herbal references inhabited a narrow bookcase there. I sipped my tea and perused the titles, selecting two which I knew included information about specific herbs to avoid during pregnancy.

Light washed across the ceiling.

I turned. The source came from the end of the alley. Something made me switch off the lamp and stand there in the dark.

Watching.

Headlights crept into view. A car crawled down the alley, bumping on the uneven track so the light bobbed gently across the back fence. Visible bit by bit through the slats, it was nonetheless impossible to make out an outline. The beams were low to the ground—a car rather than a truck or SUV.

Terror arrowed through me, so surprising it made me gasp. I couldn't move for a long moment after the car was gone, the big windows in my workroom that I loved so much now causing me to feel exposed and vulnerable.

I forced myself to take a step.

And then another.

It was only a car in the alley. No reason to have such a strong reaction, Sophie Mae. Hormones. Must be PMS hormones.

Great.

Shaking it off, I checked all the window and door locks even though I knew Kelly had already done that, and went back up to the main level of the house. All the calming effects of the chamomile tea had vanished.

A small noise drifted to my ears as I passed the hallway. I stopped, listening hard. Erin's bedroom was the closest, and I was pretty sure it had come from inside the closed door. It sounded almost like a bird—yet not quite. Only silence greeted my straining ears. After a few minutes, I moved on to the stairs and up to our quarters.

Still too tense to join Barr in bed, I drifted through the arched doorway into our sitting room. Once a guest bedroom, it now contained a loveseat and recliner, bookshelves and a roll-top desk where we completed our personal correspondence, paid bills, and so on. A small bouquet of pink sweet peas decorated the coffee table, a vague outline in the dark. Their spicy scent filled the small space, and I breathed it in. Opening the wooden blinds, I settled into the comfy recliner by the window and watched the wind push the clouds across the sky. The Krazy Kat clock that Barr had mounted on the wall ticked loudly in the silence.

Movement on the street outside drew my eye. Someone on the sidewalk across from the house. My blood pressure began to rise, and I half stood, clutching the window sill. Relief winged through me as I recognized the tall figure—and the dog—strolling past. Bette, out walking Alexander. I glanced at the clock, its tail pendulum swinging back and forth. It was almost two-thirty in the morning. Not the most common time to walk your dog, but Bette was an *artiste*, and sometimes kept odd hours.

Better than sitting and stewing all night, like I was. Of course, she had Alexander to keep her company. I might be able to steal Brodie away from Erin—and tonight Clarissa—but he did not offer the comfortable safety of a powerful German shepherd. I watched the big dog's tail arching through the air as he strode confidently beside his owner. She stopped and ran her fingers through the ruff around his neck, and then bent as if to whisper something in his ear before moving on.

That woman loved her dog.

And she'd loved her mother. I'd held the notion of her realistic clay masks in the back of my mind ever since we'd talked about them, worrying at the idea of one of Barr like Brodie worried a bone. Her comments had made me think about what it would be like to have a mask of my husband if anything happened to him. Which, of course, made me think of things happening to him.

I'd always worried about that a bit, especially given his line of work, but my confidence in Barr's ability to deal with any situation assuaged my concerns. Now we were talking about bringing a new member into the family, and that put a whole new spin on it. And unlike some newlyweds, I knew bad things could happen. After all, I'd already lost one husband.

Musing, I watched our friend and neighbor walk her dog out of my line of sight, heading for home. Maybe it was time for me to head to bed and get some much needed sleep.

Outside, a car drove down the street. I wouldn't have paid much attention, except it was moving so slowly.

Like the one in the alley.

Then the headlights went out, and the car came to a standstill in front of our house.

The hair on the back of my neck flexed to attention, and I leaned forward again, almost pressing my nose against the window glass.

The moonlight revealed a familiar outline. A Camaro. A red Camaro, in fact.

Hallie.

TWENTY-FIVE

I OPENED MY MOUTH to shout, then snapped it shut. No need to panic the entire household. Barr and I could handle this. Jumping to my feet, I began to turn when another movement outside caught my eye.

Clarissa, ghostly in a scanty white nightgown, tiptoed barefoot across the yard toward the front gate.

"Barr! Wake up, Barr!" I shouted at the top of my lungs. Downstairs Brodie started barking, high yips of alarm that echoed through the house.

Heart throbbing against my ribs, I opened the window with a jolt. "Clarissa, get back inside."

She craned her head to see where the voice was coming from.

"Right now, get back into the house right now."

The driver's side door of the Camaro opened.

I flew into the hallway, almost knocking down my husband.

"What the hell is going on?" he asked, irritation cooling his voice.

“Hallie’s out front, and Clarissa’s in the yard!”

“Damn!” And he was down the stairs, me right behind him. The hall light popped on, and Meghan stumbled out of her bedroom, followed by Kelly. Barr wrenched open the door and we barreled outside.

Clarissa reached the gate and began to push it open. The porch light flicked on, illuminating the scene like a museum tableau. Hallie’s head jerked up. Fear burned in her eyes. She didn’t appear to be drunk anymore, but she was most certainly frightened half out of her wits.

“How could you?” she yelled at Clarissa, who looked confused and hurt. Barr blew by me.

“What did I do?” Clarissa asked in a plaintive voice.

Barr vaulted the short fence. Hallie scrambled into her car and it roared to life. She yelled out the window. “How could you tell them I was coming for you? I thought you were on my side.”

“I am!” the girl protested as I reached her.

Barr leaped back as the Camaro took off, nearly running over his foot. He ran a couple of steps, then whirled and loped back to where Meghan and Kelly stood on the porch, Erin hovering next to them. They parted to let him inside, and Meghan hurried down the steps.

Hallie decelerated, possibly not wanting to call attention to herself in the quiet streets. I watched the taillights move sedately down the block. This was the third time that woman had pulled something crazy, and the third time she’d gotten away. I swore under my breath.

Clarissa looked up at me.

"Sorry," I said. And promptly swore again.

"Come on, honey," Meghan said from behind us. I turned as she held out her hand to Clarissa. Over her shoulder, I spied Erin's bicycle leaning against the side of the house, under the eaves.

"Open the gate," I yelled, running to the bike as fast as my ducky slippers could carry me. I hopped on and pedaled awkwardly across the grass. Erin and Kelly looked on open-mouthed as I passed.

Meghan got the gate open just in time. Pumping hard, I jumped the curb with a jolt that made my teeth rattle in my skull. I steered the bike down the street in the direction I'd seen the Camaro last, thankful for the slight decline.

Bette was in her front yard, peering up toward our house as I blasted by. Alexander wagged his tail. She said something, but the rush of the night air drowned out her words.

There. Red dots in the night. I pedaled harder, legs burning. I forced myself to keep going. *Left, right, left, right.*

The lights got bigger.

And then they turned right. I was still at least two blocks away from her.

At the next intersection, I veered around the corner and almost ran smack dab into a small pickup stopped in front of a house. Swerving shy of its bumper, I thanked the powers that be Cadyville rolled up the sidewalks early, and they mostly stayed rolled until dawn. For the most part, I wouldn't have to worry about traffic.

But neither would Hallie.

I worked my way diagonally through the streets toward where the Camaro would be if Hallie kept going straight after she turned.

I cut down an alley, moving fast, checking between houses, on the watch for moving headlights. At the corner I paused and peeked around a tall backyard fence. Blood throbbed through my veins. My ragged breath sounded loud in my own ears.

Nothing on this street. Maybe the next one over.

A fury of barking and snarling erupted on the other side of the fence. My heart, already pumping like mad, nearly sprang from my chest.

Sheesh.

I turned right and pedaled on. Behind me the disgruntled dog ran up and down its property line, sounding like a Baskerville hound. I felt rather than saw a light go on in the house.

So much for staying under the radar.

Hallie had no idea I was tracking her, and I wanted to keep it that way. My hip was still tender from her earlier blow, and another confrontation could only net me grief. My only goal on this two-wheeled jaunt was to see where she went, to keep tabs on her for as long as possible so the police would have an idea which direction she had headed. Barr must have gone back into the house to get his car keys, and help would soon be on the way. A phone would have been a good idea, but oh, well. Where would I have put it anyway?

And that was when I realized I wasn't wearing any pants.

The Victoria's Secret boy shorts were almost like real shorts, I tried to tell myself. At least Barr's ratty old sweatshirt covered my rear end. Mostly. It certainly explained why Erin's bicycle seat was so freaking uncomfortable.

I heard an engine coming up from behind me.

Barr had caught up. *Finally.* I turned to wave him in the direction I thought Hallie had gone.

But it wasn't my dearly beloved at all.

I'd zigzagged too efficiently, and come out ahead of the Camaro.

Oh, crap.

I wove toward the other side of the street, hoping she wouldn't recognize me.

Right.

Another car turned onto the street behind her. It accelerated and I craned to look over my shoulder, hoping against hope this time my husband had caught up. Hallie was driving too close to the bike for comfort, but she wasn't looking at me. Her attention focused entirely on the rearview mirror. I recognized the silhouette of a Cadyville police prowler and let out a sigh of relief.

The lightbar on top of the second vehicle flashed. Hallie tromped on the gas. The sports car sashayed toward me, and I tried to pedal faster, scanning for an open parking spot on the street.

There.

I veered directly into the narrow spot. My front wheel hit the curb. My teeth banged together, and the whole back end of the bike flipped up in the air. The sound of scraping metal filled the night as I flew arse over teakettle, tumbled over the grassy verge and public sidewalk, and stopped by bouncing off a neatly trimmed boxwood hedge. Lights came on in the hedge-owner's house.

The ground felt steady beneath me. Comfortable, if not soft. I stared up at the clouds. The wind was still pushing them along, more and more of them now. In fact, it was getting kind of chilly out. A raindrop hit my face. My feet were freezing.

"Sophie Mae! Damn it, Sophie Mae. Are you all right?"

Against my will, reality came flooding back. I was lying on a public sidewalk. In the middle of the night. Wearing my underwear and an oversized sweatshirt. My husband loomed over me, as did three or four strangers. And my butt really, really hurt.

"Where are my slippers?" I asked.

TWENTY-SIX

"You bruised your coccyx, but other than a few other minor contusions, you're fine."

I cannot express how awful it was to have Jake Beagle examine my coccyx. But he was pulling all-night duty at the Cadyville Walk-In Clinic, so I didn't have much choice. It wasn't that I didn't like Jake. I did. It was just that I knew Jake, and frankly, having a friend look at your broken behind is somehow worse than having a stranger do it.

"Bruised? Not fractured? Because it feels fractured to me," I said. The acrid smell of disinfectant was giving me a headache.

"I don't think so." He probed one more time with surprisingly gentle fingers.

I winced.

He stepped back. "Okay. You can get dressed now."

Which consisted of tugging the scrubs he'd let me borrow up over my hips.

"I can order an x-ray if you want," he said. "But that might not show a fracture even if there is one. The bruise is already visible, and probably goes to the bone."

Ow.

"It's not like we could put a splint on it, you know."

"Very funny."

"How did you get that other bruise? The one on your hip?"

"Surprisingly, it's from the same source," I said, deliberately vague.

His eyebrows knitted. "I thought you fell off your bike. Though why you'd be out riding a bike this time of night in those clothes, I can't figure. Especially since you're not exactly the sporty type."

I gave him a hard look, designed to back him off.

Which he completely ignored. "Seriously. What were you doing?"

Covering my face with my hands, I shook my head. "There's no way I can explain without sounding like an idiot."

"Eh. Wouldn't be the first time."

"What kind of bedside manner is that?" I was too tired to protest more. I wanted to sit down in the worst way. Unfortunately, all sitting was in the worst way—on my tailbone, or on my hip.

"Let me guess. It had something to do with Darla Klick's death."

I dropped my hands. "So you did know her. I knew it!"

Holding up his palms. "Everyone knows her name now. It was in the *Eye* this morning."

"But she was your patient, right? Didn't you look up her records when you found out who she was?"

He tsked. It sounded funny coming from such a big guy. Fake, too. "Why would you think that?" he said.

"Well, for one thing, you told me," I said. "At the farm you thought you recognized her from your practice. You also recommended Meghan's massage therapy to her four years ago. I know that because Meghan checked her records once we knew Darla's name."

His jaw set.

I waved my hand in the air. "Relax. I'm exhausted and cranky and my backside is throbbing like the dickens. I'm not going to ask you to reveal patient information. If it comes to that, Barr can deal with the legalities and permissions headache. Besides, I already know about her pregnancy and its sad outcome."

Jake's eyes widened. "Good Lord, Sophie Mae. Stop your search for justice, or whatever you call it, and go home. Take this ibuprofen—" He handed me a paper packet with two tablets in it. "—ice your coccyx for twenty minutes, and get some sleep. You can dive back in tomorrow." He looked at the watch on his hairy wrist. "Or at least later today."

"Isn't there something else I can do?" I almost kept the whiny note out of my voice, but not quite.

"Sorry. For something like this the treatment is mostly to grin and bear it."

Great.

Barr was waiting for me in the tiny lobby. He stood when I came out. "Did I hear him say 'ice your coccyx'?"

"Shut up." I pushed the door open and limped toward the Rover.

He hurried to my side and put his hand under my elbow for support. It felt good to breathe the cool, early morning air. The sky was overcast, and the breeze held a hint of moisture. I shivered in my borrowed sweatshirt and scrubs.

Barr hadn't gone inside the house to get his keys to go after Hallie after all. He'd guessed she was heading toward the highway, and alerted the single officer who patrolled Cadyville in the wee hours where to look for her. When Meghan told him I'd ridden off on Erin's bike, he'd come to look for me in the Land Rover. He was being really nice, too, after that one outburst when he'd found me. I'd expected him to yell at me more.

Now he said, "I'd pick you up and carry you, but that might hurt even more."

"That's okay. Jake gave me booties." I looked up just in time to see Barr get his face under control. "Go ahead. Laugh."

His mouth twitched.

"Go ahead."

"Booties," he snorted.

And suddenly, it really was pretty funny.

I didn't laugh long, though. The ibuprofen hadn't kicked in yet, and I had to perch sideways on one hip in order to bear the ride home. The adrenalin had worn off, my thighs felt like jelly, and I kept remembering the terror I'd felt when the car had driven through the alley behind our house.

Sure, it had probably been Hallie scoping out the place, but I didn't scare easily. Something about Darla's murder had wriggled deep under my usually tough hide. I'd felt compassion for victims before, as well as passion for finding their killers, but this was something new. Was it because I knew she'd been buried alive? Was it the cumulative effect of being close to so many deaths? Or had I simply managed to scare myself? The thought bothered me more than I liked to admit. I always thought if you looked up the word "practical" in the dictionary, you'd find my picture beside it.

What the heck was the matter with me? I glanced at the battered bicycle in back of the Rover. Erin was not going to be happy.

"So you caught her?" I asked, meaning Hallie. A few big raindrops splatted against the windshield.

"Patrol pulled her over right after she hit that car," Barr said, turning the wipers on low. "She complied, though she wasn't exactly friendly. She says she wasn't going to take Clarissa, that she only wanted to talk to her about what happened earlier in the afternoon. She was afraid she'd scared her."

"She did. She scared all of us. Do you believe her? That she wasn't going to try to take Clarissa?"

He shrugged and flipped his turn signal. Never mind that there wasn't another car in sight. "I don't know. While you were in with Jake, Zahn called. He says Allie's at the station, and she believes her."

"Is Hallie in jail?"

"Well, we don't technically have a jail, but yes, we're holding her at the station. If the hospital doesn't press charges—and I doubt they will—we'll have to come up with another reason to keep her until we figure out why she's behaving so strangely."

"How about attempted homicide? She tried to run me down."

"She swears that was an accident, that she didn't even see you."

I let out a disgruntled puff of air. "It's possible. I saw her eyes glued to the car coming up behind her. She didn't seem to be paying attention to me at all."

Barr glanced over at me. "It's a good thing you managed to get out of the way."

I couldn't read his expression. Was he more upset with me than I'd thought? "Why wouldn't the hospital press charges?" I asked.

He gave a kind of facial shrug. "She didn't really do anything there. A little disruption, but then she left of her own accord. Why would they bother with the legal hassle?"

"She was driving drunk, you know. At least she was earlier."

"But tonight she only blew .03. There's no actual evidence of earlier inebriation except you smelled tequila on her breath."

"We could all tell she'd been drinking," I protested.

"But there's no evidence. I need evidence."

"Speaking of evidence, you haven't found any at all that she killed Darla?"

"None. We even went back out and went through all the tools again, just in case we'd missed the weapon there, hidden in plain sight."

My head was beginning to pound in time with the throbbing of my poor tailbone. "Again?"

"Today, with Luminol. Tom and Allie let us search their house as well as Nate's trailer, since they own it." He grimaced. "We found nothing."

I stared at him. "Why didn't you tell me all this before?"

"I didn't know I had to report everything the Cadyville Police Department does to my wife."

"Don't be silly," I said. "That isn't what I meant at all. Only that if I'm going to be of any use to you I need to know things." I could hear the stridency in my voice, but I couldn't seem to stop it. My patience felt like a brittle husk waiting to crumble at the slightest touch.

PMS. Or, more likely, just a really crappy night.

"Okay, first off, there was nothing to tell. That's my point," Barr said. His patience was wearing thin, too. I couldn't blame him. "And secondly, you are hereby put out to pasture."

"What? Barr—"

"What would you have done if that test had come out positive tonight? Would you still have hopped on a bicycle and ridden off after a murder suspect in the wee hours of the morning?" He was practically shouting now.

I burst into tears.

Barr pulled up in front of the house and came around to my side of the car. He helped me out, and we stood there for a few minutes in the light rain until I got my act together.

"I'm sorry," I snuffled.

"No, I'm sorry."

"I hate it when we fight."

He laughed.

I pulled away and looked at him. "What?"

"If that was a fight, I think we're in pretty good shape."

TWENTY-SEVEN

It turned out that a brisk, nocturnal bike ride, an involuntary back flip, and a visit with an old doctor friend before tumbling into bed at four o'clock in the morning was an excellent cure for insomnia. However, the morning after sucked.

I awoke alone, blinking blearily at the daylight pushing in around the bedroom curtain. It looked bright and yellow, so the clouds from the night before had blown through. The clock on my bedside table read seven-thirty. Only three and a half hours of sleep, and without even moving I could tell the day was going to be painful. I lay on my left side, and my coccyx throbbed in time with my heart. But it was my own fault for chasing after Hallie.

Buck up, Sophie Mae. Time to get going.

Easier thought than done, but I managed. Gritting my teeth, I swung my feet to the floor, only to discover my ducky slippers, a bit muddy and worse for the previous night's wear, sitting by the bed. Standing didn't feel too bad. I tentatively stretched my arms toward the ceiling. So far so good.

I made my way gingerly down the hallway to the bathroom. After a dose of ibuprofen and a long, hot shower with invigorating, rosemary-scented soap, I rubbed a generous application of arnica salve on my bruises. Then I dressed at half speed, amazed at how little damage I'd suffered, especially considering how little I'd been wearing on my lower half.

At least the photographer from the *Cadyville Eye* hadn't had a chance to catch my antics on camera. Neighborhood gossips would have to fill the bill in that regard. Unless one of them had gone digital and had already posted pictures of my scantily clad posterior around the Internet.

What a lovely thought.

I dressed in my softest, well-worn jeans. They had a big hole in the knee, but I wasn't aiming for sartorial splendor today. Bette and I were scheduled to volunteer at the Turner Farm this morning, and bruised tailbone or not, I had no intention of letting Tom and Allie down. Adding a worn, Hard Rock Miami T-shirt I'd bought at the thrift store and a pair of sturdy work boots to my ensemble, I opened the door of our quarters and prepared to embrace the day.

The mouthwatering smell of bacon greeted me, and I discovered Meghan and Erin at the kitchen table, murmuring with their heads together. Brodie lay with his head on Erin's foot. They all looked up when I entered.

"How are you feeling?" Meghan asked. Wearing a bright yellow sundress, she looked fresh as a proverbial daisy after so little sleep.

"A little tender, but okay. Where's Clarissa?" I headed for the coffee pot as if it were an oasis in the Sahara. A plate of bacon and buttered toast beckoned from the counter beside it. I grabbed a piece of each and poured a steaming mug of dark roast.

"The Turners picked her up before you got back from your little adventure last night. This morning. Whatever," Meghan said. "I called them as soon as Barr left to go after you. They were here within fifteen minutes."

And Barr and I had been so tired when we got home we hadn't even asked about the teenaged object of Hallie's nocturnal visit. Meghan and Kelly had been sitting on the sofa waiting for us, but no one had been in much of a mood for conversation. I'd assumed Clarissa was back in Erin's bedroom, and within minutes we'd all retired to our respective rooms.

Leaning my uninjured hip against the counter, I paused before taking my first much-needed sip of caffeine. "So Allie must have gone to the station after that. Barr told me last night she believes her sister. Hallie's story is that she only wanted to talk to Clarissa about that weird scene yesterday afternoon." I glanced at Erin. "I wonder if Allie thought her twin might be the ... you know."

"Murderer?" she piped up.

"I have no idea," Meghan said. "I didn't get that impression from her, though. She seemed just as anxious to get her sister home as her daughter."

My bet was that Tom didn't share his wife's concern.

"Why do you say that anyway?" Meghan asked.

I wasn't going to go into all the reasons for Hallie being Darla's killer and Nate's attacker, not with Erin staring at me like a cat looks at a bird, so I stuck with the most obvious. "They wanted us to look after Clarissa away from the farm so she'd be safe. I wondered whether they might suspect one of their own. But now that Hallie is in jail, they've taken their daughter back."

Meghan shrugged. "After all the hoopla here, they probably just want Clarissa home with them."

I looked at Erin. "Will you miss her?"

"No." The word was decisive.

I raised one eyebrow.

"She read part of my book last night while I was asleep!"

"Ohh ... and you haven't let any of us see it."

"That's because it's not ready. I didn't give her permission or anything. She read my story in the middle of the night when I was asleep, and then before her parents came to get her she said it was silly!"

"She'd had a hard night. Maybe she was just lashing out," Meghan said.

"Whatever." At least Erin didn't seem fazed by the criticism.

I swallowed a bite of bacon. "Bug, how did Clarissa know Hallie was outside? Was she watching for her?"

"I told you—I was asleep. But I bet her aunt texted her on her *cell phone*." She shot a look at her mother. "Clarissa told me they did that all the time."

"Was she texting before you guys went to sleep?"

"I don't know. Her phone made a noise once."

"What did it sound like?"

"Kind of a little *doink doink*."

That might have been the sound I'd heard. But if Hallie was already in contact with Clarissa, why did she go to all the trouble to drive to our house unless she really did want her niece to go with her?

"So where's my bike?" Erin asked. "Mom said you wrecked it."

"Yeah, the frame's all bent up. I'm sorry, Bug, I really am. I'll get you a brand new one, okay?"

"Okay!"

"I bet the old one can be fixed," Meghan said, sounding cheerful as all get out.

"No, I want to get her a new one," I said. Why was my housemate grinning like that? Something was up.

Squinting, I asked, "What were you two whispering about when I came in?"

A big grin split Erin's face, all thought of Clarissa and her boundary issues forgotten. "Show her, Mom."

"Show me what, Mom?" I asked.

Meghan's face held quiet pleasure. She held out her hand.

It took a moment for the ring to register. When it did, I sank carefully onto the edge of a chair opposite her and took her hand in mine to examine it more closely. It was a deep blue sapphire in an antique platinum setting. The style and colors were so perfectly Meghan the ring could have sprouted right out of her finger.

"When did this happen?" I asked.

"Last night. After we—" She glanced at Erin. "After everyone went to bed."

"I thought you ... I'm confused."

"Kelly asked *me* to marry *him* last night. He'd been waiting until the ring was done. He designed it himself."

My mouth dropped open, and I laughed. "That's fabulous! Oh, honey, I'm so thrilled for you. Talk about two people who think alike."

She grinned at me, and I grinned back, and then we both grinned at Erin for a while.

"Have you set a date?" I asked.

"We're going to Vegas in two weeks."

"You're kidding."

"Erin's going to come with us, and we want you and Barr to come, too. Can Cyan take care of Winding Road?"

"Um, I guess so. Let me check in with her. After all, school will be starting some time in there. Why the hurry?" And as the last words came out, my eyes widened in question.

My housemate waved away the notion. "Nothing like that. We just want to get going with our lives. Plus, I saw what happens if you wait. My mother would swoop down on us and then Kelly's would get involved. She's nice, really, but a bit domineering, if you know what I mean."

"More than my mother?"

"Maybe not. But we're not taking any chances. And as for school, we'll be back before then. Bug, you're going to have to have Zoe show your chickens at the Fair, or wait until next year. Is that okay?"

Erin nodded. "Next year is fine. Can I wear another pretty dress like I did at Sophie Mae's wedding?"

"Of course."

Her comment made me think of Clarissa again. "Do you like girly girl dresses?"

Erin looked coy as one shoulder rose and dropped. "Sometimes. But mostly I want to look nice for Mom and Kelly."

No matter how much she rebelled, that kid loved her mother to pieces.

TWENTY-EIGHT

"How're you feeling, hon?" The words were right, but Barr sounded distracted.

"A little tired, but I'm okay. It looks like I missed your call?" I'd been up in our bathroom, icing my coccyx and then applying another layer of arnica salve when he'd telephoned. That stuff was already working wonders on my hip bruise. Now I was down in my workroom, making sure everything was in order before I took off for the farm. Cyan and Kalie had the day off because they'd be working the Thursday evening farmers market later.

"Right. Just wanted to let you know the hospital called. Nate's coming around."

Relief gusted through me, and I sagged against the wall. "That's terrific! Has he said anything you can use yet?"

"It sounds like he's still kind of out of it. Confused. Sergeant Zahn and I will go talk to him in a few hours."

"Not now?" I couldn't keep the disappointment out of my voice.

"He's not quite lucid yet, so it wouldn't do much good to question him now. Plus we've got another interview to get through."

"Oh, dear. You don't sound very happy about that."

"Remember the guy I told you about who had some sketchy work history? Zahn checked into it. He was working undercover for a couple of years in Albuquerque. The sergeant really likes him, so he wants us both to talk to him again."

"Zahn likes him—but you don't, necessarily?"

"He's . . . I shouldn't say anything."

"Yes, you should."

"Believe me, you'll get an earful if anything pans out from this."

I let it go. "What about Hallie? Does she know Nate's awake?"

"We haven't told her, but she does keep asking about him. At least she's not going anywhere for a while. If we have to, we'll charge her with something. Anything."

"Erin thinks Hallie was texting Clarissa last night."

"Really . . . yeah, we might be able to do something with that." He paused, then I heard him say, "I'm on my way," to someone else. "I've got to go, hon. Talk to you later, okay?"

I hesitated. Should I tell him I was going out to Turner Farm?

"Love you," he said. "'Bye." He hung up.

That answered that.

I went back upstairs to where I'd left my tote on the bench by the front door. The torn piece of paper where Daphne had scribbled her cell number was tucked into a side pocket. I punched the numbers in as I returned to my workroom.

She answered on the third ring.

"Hey, Daphne. It's Sophie Mae. How are you holding up?"

"Much better now. Nate's awake!" Then I heard her whisper, "It's Sophie Mae."

"Barr told me. That's great news. Is Faith there with you?"

"We've been here all night. Now that Nate's better, I think we might go to my house and get some sleep. Come back later in the afternoon."

"So he's going to be okay?"

"It will take some time for him to recover completely, but the doctors are very pleased. They've moved him out of the ICU."

"Excellent. Is there still an officer there?"

"How did you—oh, of course. Barr told you. Officer Dawson went home this morning."

That could be because Hallie was no longer a threat. It could also simply be because the department wasn't big enough to provide a full-time guard for Nate.

"I don't suppose he's said anything about his attacker?" Couldn't hurt to ask.

She hesitated. "No, he hasn't. He doesn't remember."

"Barr mentioned that he's still a little confused."

Another pause. "He's not confused so much as he has a blank spot."

"Blank spot?"

"In his memory. Nate doesn't understand why he's in the hospital at all. See, he doesn't remember being attacked at all. The last thing he remembers is being in his trailer."

"Oh, no."

"It shouldn't last, though," she hurried to reassure me. "The neurologist says he's seen this before. Over time Nate's memory should come back."

I urged her to get some sleep and hung up.

Over time? How much time?

Erin's voice drifted through my workroom window. Zoe had agreed to take care of the hens while we were in Las Vegas, and Erin was conducting Chickens 101 out in the backyard. Meghan sat on a stool at the main work island while I stood and mixed up a batch of massage oil scented with cedarwood and clove essential oils. The combination made me think of the coming fall and the holidays beyond that.

"Of course I'm going to the farm this morning," I said. "Tom and Allie need the help."

"They'll understand if you can't come. You were up all night trying to protect their daughter, after all."

"Oh, gosh, Megs. They could lose that place because of Darla Klick's murder. The farm's associated with violence and death now. Yesterday's volunteers canceled on them, and this is the busiest time of the season. I just can't let them down."

"Okay, then let me go in your place," Meghan said.

"Don't you have clients today?" I measured out a teaspoon of clove oil and added it to the cedarwood already in the bottle.

"I can cancel."

"That's silly."

"Stay home and take care of yourself," she insisted.

"You are not going to lose business on my account."

"You just can't stand the thought of not doing something. Fine. Stay down here and make soap or something. Boss Cyan and Kalie around for a while. But working in the field is too much."

"Listen. I know you have my best interests at heart. I do. And I appreciate that. My so-called injuries are a pain in the patootie, literally, but they're not anything serious."

Her frown lines deepened with worry.

"Besides, there's no one to boss. The girls have the day off." Using a funnel, I filled the rest of the bottle with jojoba oil.

"Hallie could be back home by now. She's already hurt you twice. I do not want you to go out there. If you insist, I'll call Barr."

"You'll . . . are you kidding me?" I spluttered. It was like threatening to tell my father. "Well, go ahead. And he'll tell you Nate woke up this morning, and they're still holding Hallie at the station."

Her eyes widened. "Nate identified her?"

"Well, not exactly. He's having some problems with his memory. Should be temporary, though."

The frown returned.

"I'll be fine."

"Do what you want." She slid off the stool. "You always do anyway. But I have a bad feeling. I can't tell you why, but I do. I wish you'd listen to me once in a while." And my best friend stomped upstairs.

I stared after her. Meghan didn't get her "feelings" very often, but when she did something was usually off.

Off, but not necessarily dangerous. Hallie was still in the holding cell at the police station. Nate was getting better. The Turners desperately needed some help. And it wasn't like I'd be working alone.

No, I wouldn't. I'd make sure of that. Whatever Tom needed us to do today, Bette and I would do it together.

"You stay here and be a good boy." Bette's braid swung over her shoulder as she bent down and stroked the big dog's head. He grinned up at her, panting his agreement. She scratched him one last time behind the ears before shutting the gate and striding out to the street.

"Alexander is always a good boy," I said as she folded her tall form into the Rover's passenger seat. At least the clay spatter on her hiking pants and tank top seemed to be dry. "I don't know that I've ever known such a well-trained dog."

She gazed fondly out the open window. He stood by the front gate, faithfully awaiting his mistress' return. "I'd like to bring him out to the farm, but I'm afraid he'll chase the chickens." She fastened her seat belt and leaned back.

"True." I laughed. "That kind of self-control might be asking a bit too much of him." I pulled away from the curb and made a U-turn south.

"Oh, he could learn. Alex is awfully smart, and he aims to please."

"I saw you out walking him last night." I might as well be the one to bring up the early morning hours.

"Hmm. I have periods of insomnia. I saw you out and about, too." Her eyes cut my way.

Taking a deep breath, I told her about both of Hallie's visits to our house, explaining how I didn't want her to get away again and leaving out the reason for the soft pillow installed under my posterior. If I leaned a wee bit to the left, away from my sore hip, driving was manageable if not pleasant. She listened to my tale with a growing expression of astonishment.

"You chased her on your bike?"

"Erin's bike, actually. And not so much chase as … track, I guess. Unfortunately, she panicked when she saw the cop car and kind of ran me off the road."

"Oh, Sophie Mae, you could have been really hurt."

I shifted on the pillow. "I'm fine. She didn't hit me with the car or anything. In fact, I'm pretty sure she was just trying to get away." Again.

"You're crazy, you know that?"

I glanced at her, expecting her to be smiling, but her face was solemn as a nun's. So I simply nodded and left it at that. "She's in custody now."

"They arrested her?"

"Not yet. They could probably come up with some charges, but for now they can keep her there while they wait."

She looked confused.

"See, it's possible she's responsible for the attacks at the farm. Nate should be able to tell us soon." I hoped. "Since she's scampered before, they want to keep an eye on her until they find out what he has to say."

"So … there's good news about Nate?" she asked.

"Yes! Really good news. He's awake now. A little off kilter still, but conscious."

She tipped her head to one side. "He's going to be okay, then."

"It sounds like it. The doctors are happy with his progress. It was touch and go there for a while."

Bette faced forward again and nodded. "That's great. His family must be so relieved."

"I met his mother yesterday. She told me a bit about Nate's background. Did you know he was raised in a commune up on Camano Island? Faith—that's his mom's name—was one of the original founders."

"Commune? How very seventies. Has he told the police who hit him?"

"Not yet. I spoke to Daphne this morning, and she told me he's having some memory problems. But the doctors say that should get better. There's been an officer there all night." I didn't mention that was for protection as much as anything.

Out of the corner of my eye I saw her shoulders lower as if she could finally relax. Like everyone else, she'd been nervous about working at the farm today. At least she'd had the guts to go anyway. If only Nate would hurry up and remember, we'd soon know the truth about what happened to him—and maybe to Darla Klick as well. At least Hallie wasn't running around loose. Yet.

TWENTY-NINE

Tom came out to meet us when I pulled into the gravel lot at the farm, looking harried and tired. Even his overalls, hanging limply on his lanky frame, appeared exhausted.

"Thank God you two showed up," he said. "No one would come out yesterday, and the guys scheduled for tomorrow just called and bailed on us. With Nate in the hospital, I'm short handed as it is." He ran his palm over his face. "Sorry. That must sound pretty insensitive. I only meant—"

I held up my hand. "We know what you meant. I talked to Daphne this morning, and she said he's doing a lot better. They've moved him out of the ICU."

We exchanged a long look, but neither of us brought up his sister-in-law. Bette, standing with her hands on her hips and looking toward the pumpkin patch, didn't seem to notice.

"I spoke briefly with him on the phone," Tom said. "He still sounds groggy, but thank the good Lord he's going to be all right. He's a good guy, you know?"

Bette and I murmured our agreement.

"Okay, then," he said, rubbing his hands together. "There's a pile of things to do. Why don't you start with harvesting green beans—they'll be too big if we wait for distribution day and will stay fresh in the cooler—and then the cucumbers. Same thing. The pickling cukes are priority, because if they get too big, no one will be able to use them."

Bette's nod was brisk, the picture of efficiency. "You've got it. We'll check in when we're done to see what else you have for us to do."

We loaded bushel baskets into the back of the second yard cart. The other one was still out where I'd found Nate the day before, no doubt covered with crows feasting on popcorn. I added a folding step stool since I wasn't as tall as Bette, and we rattled down the path toward the towering bean teepees. We went through the gate that separated the rows of vegetables from fowl and swine and trundled past the herb bed. The oregano and basil had begun to flower, and the plants were crawling with happy bees. Their low drone whispered behind us as we continued on.

Down the hill, near the farm house, Allie worked at her large potting bench, transplanting what I guessed were fall starts of broccoli, cauliflower, cabbage, and the like. She didn't look up, and her hands flew. Everything needed to be done in a hurry right now or it wouldn't get done at all. I was happy to see Clarissa appeared to be helping her mother.

We passed by the raspberry canes. Weeds crawled beneath, and ripe berries begged to be plucked and eaten. I couldn't bear the thought of those raspberries going to waste. As we continued on, my companion eyed the yellow tape that still festooned the popcorn field. She didn't say anything, so I didn't either.

At the end of the row of bean poles we stopped, and I craned my neck back. "Oh, boy. Look at all those. We might be here for a while." The forty-foot row of pyramidal structures was seven feet high in places, and absolutely covered with the clinging vines of heirloom pole beans—a variety amusingly called Lazy Wife because they were stringless.

Bette's lips curved into a smile as she closed her eyes and tipped her face to the sky. "That's okay. It's a glorious day. There won't be many more of them."

"No kidding. The rain will be here soon enough."

We set to work, picking fast and dropping the ripe cylinders into the baskets at our feet. My tailbone quietly throbbed, but nothing else hurt. A light breeze kept the air cool as we raced along the row, and for a moment the world felt golden. I had helped grow these beans. Now I harvested them—for myself, and for other people. It was a reassuring connection to life that grounded me and provided perspective.

That feeling lasted as we worked along the first teepee, listening only to the birds and far off traffic and the rustle of cornstalks in the wind. But Zen is Meghan's thing more than mine and soon my mind had darted back to the grisly discovery of Darla's body.

"So one of the reasons I was awake last night was because I was thinking about how the killer must have buried the body in the compost pile," I said. "See, Clarissa told me Hallie doesn't do any work on the farm, and that she hates to get dirty, so that would be a strange thing to do. Burying Darla Klick in the compost, I mean. Don't you think?" I glanced over at Bette.

"Mmm," she murmured, reaching to the top of the teepee for a handful of nice-sized specimens. Plucking them, she dropped them in the basket and went back for more.

She didn't seem interested in my theories, but didn't seem to mind my thinking out loud either, so I went on. "That's one strike against it being her. On the other hand, the blows to the head didn't kill either Darla or Nate, so the idea that a woman did it makes sense. No offense to our gender, but it's a simple fact we're not as strong as men. I figure the killer planned to come back and move the body later. I mean, they couldn't think she'd stay in the compost forever, right? Unless they thought she'd eventually turn *into* compost. I suppose someone might think that if they don't know you have to turn a pile like that pretty often."

Bette had stopped picking altogether and now stared at me with huge eyes. "What do you mean—the blow to Darla's head didn't kill her?"

"Ah—that's the kind of inside information you get when your husband is a police detective. Darla Klick didn't die from blunt force trauma. She died from suffocation."

"From … from …" Now she was gaping at me.

Remembering the horrible dream I'd had right after Barr told me, I couldn't blame her. I nodded. "Whether it was on purpose or not, she was buried alive."

"That's awful," Bette whispered.

"I *know*. If it hadn't been for that, I don't think I would have involved myself with any of it."

Was that true? Maybe. Probably not. Either way, Nate would have identified Darla eventually, Clarissa still would have come to stay with us, and Hallie would still have knocked me down in the yard. I might not have tried to chase a Camaro on a bicycle, though. So there was that.

Looking over, I saw Bette had begun to pick again, but her hands were shaking so badly she could hardly hold onto the beans.

"Oh, gosh," I said. "I guess I've gotten used to the idea over the last few days. It's a creepy thing to think about, isn't it?"

So low I could hardly hear her, she whispered, "It would be like drowning."

I paused, and tipped my head. "Kind of." I eyed her. "Are you afraid of the water?"

"Terrified." Her hands continued to tremble.

Darn it. I'd totally ruined her enjoyment of the sunny day. Nice job, Sophie Mae.

"No one should ever have to drown." She dropped a double handful of beans into her basket. "It has to be the most horrible death ever. I've imagined it so many times, how it would feel, not being able to breathe."

My dream came flooding back to me. "I guess it would be like drowning." Drowning in dirt. But I didn't say that. I'd said enough.

"Head pounding, trying to wait just one more second to breathe, hoping you'll be saved, finally giving in, and there's no air, only water. Water filling your lungs, cold, so cold and still you can't breathe, even though you broke down and inhaled. And there's no going back." She stilled, and slowly her head turned until she was looking me straight in the eye. "No going back."

Standing there in the full August sun, a shiver crawled all the way down my spine. What on earth ... ? I felt the skin tighten across my face, and my mind started chugging. Fitting together what had seemed like random events over the last few days. Faster then, making connections, assembling a whole story out of bits of information. A commune, two teenagers with their lives ruined, a mask of a woman on a wall. A drowning.

The friend who had come to Happy Daze with the accident victim. Someone Leigh had been seeing for a while that Faith had only mentioned in passing, not even by name. Not even by gender.

"Bette?" I licked my lips and struggled not to look away. "Did you know someone who drowned?"

Her pupils widened, but otherwise she didn't respond.

"Someone you cared about?"

She flinched.

I took a deep breath. "Did you know Leigh? I'm sorry, I don't remember her last name."

Tears filled her eyes, spilled over, but she never looked away. We stood like that for what felt like a long time. The only sound was the hum of Tom's trackhoe on the other side of the farm and Bette's ragged breathing.

She looked off into a distance that wasn't there, into the past. "Weber. Leigh Weber. Yes, I knew her. I loved her, and they took her from me."

THIRTY

I CHOSE MY NEXT words with care. "Nate's mother told me a little about what happened. She said it was a horrible accident."

A sob ripped from her throat, and she shuddered. "If those kids hadn't been so selfish, if their parents had *thought* before sending them out in that little boat. But no, they weren't thinking about anything because they were going to have a party, a nice big party and a bonfire, with music and dancing and that was more important than making sure there were enough life jackets, more important than keeping Leigh alive."

We were alone, out in the middle of a field. Me and a killer. Allie was too far away to hear, and the engine of the John Deere would drown my call anyway. Still, I wasn't afraid, so intense was my sympathy for this woman I had called my friend, this woman who carried a grief so deep none of us had known anything about it.

"Bette," I said. "Come sit down. Here, on the step stool." I took it out of the cart and unfolded it.

Ignoring me, she gestured wide with both arms. "Happy Daze. Exactly what a bunch of idiots would call an over-romanticized place like that. *Commune.*" The word dripped with sarcasm. She sniffed and swiped at her eyes with the back of her hand, leaving a damp smudge of dirt across her temple. "More like a bunch of infantile wannabes. Dreamers. Fools. They almost starved to death the first couple years they were out there, you know. But Leigh had been friends with them in college, and she loved the place. Spent as much time as she could out on Camano Island with her friends, always threatening to join."

That jived with what Faith Snow had said.

"I would never have even considered such a thing, if it weren't for her. She took me for the weekend three different times. It was hard, hard work, just feeding themselves and staying warm. Work that took up all their time, even the kids' when they weren't in school. They said they loved it though. Leigh wanted to slow down to that kind of pace. Her job as a bank manager was stressful, and she worked long hours. I understood why she wanted to quit, I did. It was just that I needed time for my pottery, for my sculpture. My work was developing a following, and it looked like I could really make a living as an artist. I didn't want to give it up, but I would have. I would have done it all differently if only I could have her back."

Her eyes pleaded with me to understand.

Inclining my head, I said, "Tell me what happened."

"The kids, Darla and Nate, went out to pull crab pots. Leigh insisted on going with them. She said she'd done it lots of time, that it was fun."

I'd meant that I wanted her to tell me what had happened with Darla and Nate at the farm. But this was okay, too, even if I'd heard the story from Faith Snow.

"She couldn't swim worth a lick, but that didn't stop her. Leigh had lived a charmed life, and she never thought anything bad could happen to her. Said they'd been doing it for years. That there were life jackets on the boat, that I worried too much for my own good—and hers. Our last words were an argument about how I worried too much about her. She went out on that boat with those kids, and I went back to help build the bonfire." She stopped and hung her head, staring down at the dirt at her feet.

"Two hours later, Nate and Darla came back. Alive. But Leigh was gone."

My throat ached from hearing the emotion in her words, from wondering how it would feel to lose someone I loved so suddenly, so out-of-the-blue. I'd been as prepared as a wife could be when lymphoma took my first husband, and far away from home when my brother had committed suicide. What Bette had endured was a different thing altogether.

It didn't justify murder, however.

"It turned out there weren't enough life jackets." She picked a handful of beans and began snapping them off, inch-by-inch, and dropping them on the ground. "Both those kids could swim, but they took the life jackets and left her without one."

Faith had said Leigh was the adult, so she insisted the teens use the safety equipment. Bette wouldn't want to hear that right now, though.

"They should have been able to save her. I've imagined it over and over and over. I never got a chance to say goodbye."

She threw the ends of the broken green beans down and looked up. Her gaze snagged mine, and I couldn't look away. Couldn't move. My feet had grown roots down into the soil, leaving me captive to her story.

"They took her from me, and they took the chance for me to say goodbye, to tell her one last time how much I loved her. Oh, sure, they said it was an accident, but I could tell from the way they acted that something had happened. Something that shouldn't have. Their guilt followed them home like a deep brown haze." Her voice had taken on a dreamy quality. "I kept making them tell me what happened, over and over, until their parents made them stop. They said it was traumatic for their children." She grimaced. "Traumatic—for their children who were still alive and not blue and cold and gone forever.

"I lived in a fog for a while after that. Numb. Clay saved me. Art saved me. But then that crystal-clear image I had of Leigh in my mind began to fade."

"And you made a mask to remember her by," I said. "Like you did with your mother."

She nodded. "Leigh's was first, then my brother, and then my mother. I did my best to remember Leigh, to keep her alive in my heart, not to forget her. I replay memories of her every day."

Oh, Bette. That's not good. That's not right.

"Then Nate moved to Cadyville. He recognized my name from the CSA member list, and came to see me. Just showed up at my door, unannounced. I was furious. But he talked me into letting him inside, and then he told me about the terrible guilt he carried with him. He said he'd always feel guilty, as long as he lived. I could see he was haunted. After talking to him, I was upset, of course, but not as angry. I'd wanted those kids to suffer. I wanted them to pay for taking Leigh away from me. But now it seemed Nate had been paying all along. It made me feel better."

I stared at her, stunned.

She began to pace, her pent-up story spilling out in a tumble of words now. "Then months later darling Darla called me. She was staying with her parents in Arlington, and had tracked down Nate. He'd told her that I lived here in Cadyville. That he'd talked to me. She called my house, said she wanted to speak with me, too, about what had happened all those years ago."

Bette sighed, and I could feel her dread about telling me what happened next.

"I didn't want her to show up at my house like Nate had, and she was so insistent. So I suggested we meet here on Sunday night."

"Did you drive?" I blurted.

"I rode my bike," she said.

"Did you plan to kill her?"

She threw up her hands. "Of course not! Sophie Mae, don't you get it? None of this was supposed to happen. Nate told me Darla's life had been ruined when Leigh died, just like his. I wanted to see if that was true. She was supposed to apologize to me like Nate did." She stopped in front of me, her eyes boring into mine, willing me to see.

And I did see. I saw that Bette had nurtured her loss until it had grown and mutated into such a skewed view of the world that it bordered on insanity. How could this have happened right under everyone's noses? She'd always been eccentric to a degree, but we chalked that up to being an artist. On the surface, she'd always come across as pretty darn normal.

I didn't trust myself to say anything. She moved closer, too close. I could smell toothpaste on her breath. The bean teepees were behind me, so there was no place I could go without pushing her out of the way. All my instincts told me that was a bad idea, so I simply nodded and tried to hide my increasing fear.

"But she didn't apologize! Darla wasn't at all like Nate. She wasn't suffering. Oh, she said she did for a long time, until she realized she had to give up her guilt. Therapy helped her to let it go, she said, and now she could finally be happy. Happy!" She glared at me.

I tried a tentative smile. It was completely lost on her.

"How dare she be happy?" Bette raged. "And then she had the utter audacity to suggest I do the same thing. That obviously I hadn't let go of the past, and getting professional help could help me do that.

"She couldn't see that I don't *want* to let go of the past, that it would be letting go of Leigh. It made me so mad, so angry. No, mad is right. I went crazy for a minute or two, maybe only seconds, I don't know, and the next thing I knew I'd hit her with the shovel." Bette backed away and slowly spread her hands, palms up.

Asking for something, but I didn't know what.

Turning, she stepped away and gazed out over the pumpkins. I inhaled quietly, relieved to get a break from those intense eyes and her close proximity.

"When I realized what I'd done, I panicked. I took her wallet, dragged her to the compost pile, and buried her as best as I could. I thought maybe I could come back with my car and retrieve her, dump the body someplace else. But I didn't really have a plan, and the next day Meghan found her. I knew Nate would suspect me as soon as he realized it was Darla. I thought he'd just go to the police, that it was all over for me. So I kept working and waited for them to come for me."

Her shoulders slumped. "But Nate didn't call the authorities. He contacted me."

"Why?" I couldn't help asking. Blackmail was a possibility, but from what I knew of Nate it seemed out of character. Still, I didn't exactly trust my ability to judge character at the moment.

She shrugged. "I told you he felt guilty. If I didn't have anything to do with Darla's death, then he didn't want to cause me any trouble."

"He called you?"

"No. He came by my house the night of the vegetable distribution. Tuesday. Late."

After driving back from telling Darla's parents she was dead. I remembered Bette's hurry to leave that evening when I asked her to stick around. Late for a dinner date, she'd said.

Right. I wondered whether she had been expecting Nate to stop by after all.

"I tried to assure him that I didn't have any idea what he was talking about. That Darla hadn't shown up at the time we'd agreed on, so maybe she'd already been dead by then," Bette said. "But I'm not a very good liar."

Hmm. I had to disagree.

"I could tell he didn't believe me. I thought there still might be a chance to go on with my life."

By getting away with murder.

"So I took the shovel I'd hit Darla with—I'd taken it home with me so no one would find it at the farm—and followed him in my car. It was dark, and late, so I thought I could risk it. I turned my headlights off once I got to the farm turnoff, and no one saw me. He was still in his car, outside his trailer when I got there."

She cocked her head in puzzlement. "He stayed there for a while. At first I thought he might already be on the phone, but it didn't look like it. He stared straight ahead for the longest time."

Probably thinking about what to do next. Poor guy.

"Is that where you hit him? By the Airstream?" I asked without thinking. But Barr hadn't said anything about Nate being dragged, and strong as she was, I didn't think Bette could have carried him to the popcorn field. Yard cart? Could he have come to and wandered away before succumbing to his head wound?

But she shook her head. "I was afraid someone in the farmhouse would see me. So I made some noise down by the corn when he finally got out of his car. Sure enough, he thought it was raccoons or something and came down to scare them away. The shovel had worked the first time, so I hit him with it again."

"Except it didn't," I said. "Work I mean. You really did bury that poor girl alive."

She hung her head and covered her face with both hands. Sometime during her confession, Tom had finished with the trackhoe.

Now I could only hear the cries of crows in the cornfield and the quiet weeping of Bette the potter.

Careful step by careful step, I backed down the row of beans.

She dropped her hands and looked up at me through red-rimmed eyes. "What are you doing?"

I turned and ran. Footsteps pounded behind me.

"Sophie Mae! Wait! I'll come with you."

A hand fell on my shoulder. I flinched. Strong fingers dug into my shoulder, and I slowed to a stop. Faced her.

Her tears had stopped. She offered a small smile. "What's wrong?"

I blinked. "What's *wrong*?"

"Why . . . you don't think I'm going to hurt you, do you?"

Shrugging off her hand, I stepped away. "The thought had occurred to me."

"Sophie Mae, I wouldn't do that."

Right.

"I know it's over," she said. "I've always known someone would figure it out, even if Nate didn't recover. I'm glad it was you."

Just when I thought it couldn't get any weirder.

"Will you take me to the police station now?"

My lips parted in surprise. "Um, sure."

"Hang on. Let me get the beans we picked."

I watched with numb wonder as she walked back, placed the baskets into the yard cart, and pulled it to where I stood waiting. Together we walked to the farm stand and stepped inside.

THIRTY-ONE

TOM HEFTED A CRATE of freshly picked melons and turned toward us in surprise.

"I'm afraid you'll have to find someone else to take over for us," Bette said.

Irritation warred with the worry that had pinched his features ever since Meghan had stumbled on the Timberland boot in his compost pile. "What's going on?"

"I killed Darla Klick and hit Nate over the head."

He froze, darting a look at me.

I raised my eyebrows and nodded.

"I'm really sorry for all the trouble I caused you and your family. You don't have to worry about your little girl anymore—you never did. Sophie Mae is going to take me to the police station now." She turned to me. "It's a relief, really. Let's go."

In a daze, I walked to the Rover and retrieved my phone from the tote in the back seat. "I'm just going to call Barr and let him know we're coming."

She took a deep breath. "Yes. Okay."

"Barr? Are you at the station? ... Well, you're going to have to put off that interview ... I know, I know. But believe me, this is more important. I'm bringing Bette Anders in so she can officially confess to murder."

Sergeant Zahn and Detective Ambrose met us halfway to the station and escorted us through town. There were no lights, no sirens, and we didn't exceed the twenty-five-mile-an-hour speed limit once.

Beside me, Bette asked, "Do you think they'll let me have Leigh's mask in prison?"

Sudden pity surged over me, almost taking my breath away. "I don't see why not."

A few moments later she said, "I have a favor to ask."

I swallowed. "What's that?"

"I've thought about this a lot over the last few days. I'd like you to take Alexander. Will you do that for me?"

I thought of the big, gorgeous, loyal beast waiting for the woman beside me to come home. I thought of Bette, so alone except for the past and her dog and nearly burst into tears.

"Yes. We'll take good care of him. I promise," I finally managed to croak out.

"And Sophie Mae? I finished Barr's mask. It's in my studio. The front door's unlocked."

I turned into the parking lot of the small, square building on Maple Avenue that housed the Cadyville Police Department. "You knew you weren't going back home, didn't you?"

She didn't answer.

Barr opened her door then, ratcheted a pair of handcuffs onto her wrists, and Zahn took her elbow. She twisted her head to look over her shoulder. Our eyes met.

"Thank you, Sophie Mae."

I opened my mouth to speak, but then closed it again. There weren't any words to express what I felt. Nonetheless, she nodded her understanding before facing forward and marching into the building.

I watched her go inside. Barr put his arm around me, and I leaned my head against his shoulder. I wanted to cry, but no tears came. So I stared at the silver dollar holding his string tie together and blinked dry eyes.

"Sophie Mae?" His tone was gentle.

I took a deep breath and pushed away. "I'm fine."

He looked down at me with deep brown eyes full of a sweetness not many people got to see. "No, you're not."

And he was right. A friend of mine had just confessed to killing a young woman out of misplaced rage and grief and then trying to kill a nice young man because he could identify her.

A *friend.*

I liked putting together the pieces of a puzzle, figuring out human motivations and uncovering secrets. Some of those secrets had been disturbing or made me sad, but I'd thought that was the price of justice. And I'd helped to catch other killers. Some were acquaintances, some were essentially strangers, but none of them had been people I'd known for a long time, socialized with, respected, and enjoyed spending time with.

This was different.

This time was going to take some thoughtful processing. That didn't need to start in the parking lot of the police station, though. So I said, "At least you can let Hallie go now."

Barr frowned, but allowed me to change the subject. After all, he could follow up later, and would, probably ad nauseum, until he knew for sure I was all right.

"Yeah, about that," he said. "While you were harvesting vegetables and getting a murder confession, we found out a few interesting things about the evil twin."

Raising one eyebrow, I said, "Do tell."

"After you told me about Hallie texting Clarissa, Zahn got a warrant for her cell phone. Sure enough, there was a record of their exchange last night." He paused.

I made a get-on-with-it gesture.

"Apparently Clarissa had taken something that Hallie wanted. She wanted it very much."

Holy cow. "Oh, my God," I said. "Is that why she was being so weird?"

He looked stunned. "Are you telling me you knew?"

"Are you talking about the diamond drop earrings?"

Nodding, he asked, "But how …?"

"Clarissa was wearing them yesterday. She said she'd borrowed them from Hallie, but I got the feeling she didn't exactly have explicit permission to take them. She said Hallie let her borrow nice stuff all the time."

Better to ask forgiveness later than permission first.

Shrugging, I said, "I figured it was one more way dear auntie indulged her niece."

"Not exactly. See, those earrings weren't hers to loan."

Now I was confused. "Whose were they?" Surely not Allie's.

"Brother's Jewelers."

"In Monroe? But how did she ... ohhh. Really? She stole them?"

He nodded again. "We didn't find anything suspicious when we searched the Turners' house, but boy, we hit the mother lode in the trunk of her car."

"So it wasn't just the earrings?"

"You know all those shopping trips she took Clarissa on? More like shoplifting trips."

I took a step back, catching myself on the hood of the Rover. The metal was hot from the sun. "She didn't. Oh, Barr, you're not saying she involved a thirteen-year-old girl, her own *niece*, are you?"

He looked grim. "Hallie said Clarissa would distract a clerk so she could slip something in her purse. They'd become very good at it."

That explained a lot. Her focus on Clarissa, the way she manipulated her emotions, the look of terror I'd seen in her eyes the night before. She'd been afraid Clarissa would give her away.

"What a bitch," I said.

My husband barked a laugh, then caught himself.

"Poor Allie." I could only imagine what Meghan would feel like in the same situation. Or how I'd feel. That parenting thing wasn't for wimps.

Barr nodded. "You realize, of course, that if you hadn't joined the CSA and insisted on discovering Darla Klick's identity, we wouldn't know about Hallie's little enterprise."

Was he trying to make me feel better about Bette turning out to be a murderer?

"She would have been caught eventually," I said.

"I'm sure you're right. But not for a while. She'd still be taking Clarissa on 'shopping trips' and living the high life."

"And here I thought she had all that money to burn because she'd made out well in her divorce."

"We haven't had a chance to look into her finances yet, but I doubt that's the case."

"At least that explains her crazy stunts at the house." Utterly enervated, I turned toward the car door. All I wanted to do was go home and sleep until I had to help the girls get set up for the farmers market.

Wait a second. I whirled around. "But what about her obsession with Nate? Did that have anything to do with the shoplifting scheme? Could he be involved somehow?"

Barr shrugged. "It doesn't look like it. She's still asking about him, constantly. Maybe she really is in love with him and wanted him to think she was rich?"

I rubbed my eyes. "That's one messed-up woman you have in there." My hand dropped, and so did my stomach. "Actually, two messed-up women. Oh, Barr." And finally tears stung my eyelids.

THIRTY-TWO

"If you weren't in such a hurry, you could have a double wedding with Nate and Daphne," Ruth said over her shoulder. She was slicing Lazy Wife green beans into uniform lengths that would fit into wide-mouthed pint jars.

Next to her, three dozen of those sterilized jars lined our kitchen counter. Meghan dropped a sprig of dill, a small cayenne pepper, and a clove of peeled garlic into each one. I stirred a steaming pot of water, vinegar, and salt on the stovetop, its sour scent adding to the mix of flavors in the air. On another burner, water in the big, black canning pot roiled, ready to seal the first batch of dilly beans. A fan in the corner moved the humid air around the room, and I pushed a damp strand of hair off my forehead with the back of my wrist.

Erin sat at one end of the butcher block table, the tip of her tongue protruding from the corner of her mouth in concentration as she bent over her new cell phone. It was metallic yellow, and she hadn't been more than three feet away from it since Meghan had given it to her the day before.

Kelly and Barr hunched at the other end of the table, flipping through catalogs of surveillance equipment and discussing the pros and cons of subscribing to proprietary information databases. Meghan looked at me and rolled her eyes. Some of the items sounded like they'd originated in Q's laboratory.

Alexander and Brodie snoozed side-by-side in the kitchen doorway. Our new addition seemed fine during the day, but at night, sprawled on the carpet by my side of the bed, he sometimes whined in his sleep. I hoped that he'd adjust to his new living situation in time.

We'd all spent the afternoon at Turner Farm, helping Tom and Allie catch up with the backlog of work. Meghan had suggested the idea, and I'd started contacting CSA members. As soon as Jake Beagle heard our plan, he took over the phone calls. He'd talked every volunteer into showing up, plus most of the CSA members who had never worked in a garden in their lives. He'd even managed to bring in a few nonmembers to help, some of whom had bought prorated shares until the end of the year.

Bins and bags and piles of vegetables now filled the distribution shed and farm stand. We'd beaten back the worst of the weeds in most of the fields and beds, and Allie had directed a team who planted fall crops of greens, brassicas, and peas. Hallie had been released on bond, but Tom refused to allow her on the farm. With the help of Sergeant Zahn and Barr, he hadn't had any trouble taking out a restraining order to make sure his edict stuck. Clarissa, wearing overalls like her dad, had worked side-by-side with her mother. She was still snippy and whiny, but without her aunt around to confuse things she seemed more settled. I thought she'd be okay.

Allie had pulled me aside to tell me she'd convinced Hallie to get professional help. "I have to try and help her, Sophie Mae. She's my twin sister. I know deep down she's not the person you've had to deal with."

How could I judge her loyalty? I could only wish them luck.

But at the end of the day the community of Cadyville had indeed supported the Turner Farm in the spirit of CSA, and now, sunburned and tired, we settled in to preserve some of the harvest with Ruth Black's help.

"The flights are all booked to Las Vegas," Meghan said, peeling more garlic. "Tootie and Felix are coming along, too."

The two ninety-somethings had returned from Alaska full of enthusiasm for more travel, despite Tootie's constant arthritis pain.

"How about you, Ruth?" Meghan asked. "I can get a flight for you tomorrow."

The older woman frowned. "Maybe I should. I've always wanted to know what kind of trouble you can get into that needs to stay in Vegas when you leave."

I laughed.

"Bug, remember what I said about texting at the table?" Meghan asked.

Erin looked up at her mother. "We're not eating."

"We have a guest, though."

Ruth flipped her hand. "Poo. I'm not a guest."

"Sure you are." Erin put her phone in her pocket. "I'm sorry if I was rude. Can I help?"

Meghan and I exchanged glances, grateful that she'd returned to her usual sweet self.

"You could wash up the rest of those." Ruth indicated the final batch of beans in the sink with her chin.

Erin leaped up and got to work.

"When are Nate and Daphne tying the knot?" Barr tipped back in his chair and took a sip of Earl Grey tea.

"Not for a while," Ruth said. "Nate's still recovering, and they have to figure out someplace to live. He wants to be closer to the farm than Daphne's apartment, but they can't live in that little trailer."

"Is his mom still in town?" I moved to the counter and began stuffing raw beans into the jars Meghan had prepared.

"She went home a few days ago," Ruth said. "Didn't she call you?"

I nodded. "She thanked me for finding his attacker."

Ruth turned to face me, her multi-hued caftan swirling. Her cheeks glowed pink in the kitchen heat. "You know if Bette hadn't confessed to you, she could have gotten away with everything."

"Because Nate never saw who hit him?"

His memory had returned in full, but it turned out he'd never actually seen Bette sneak up behind him in the dark.

She waved her knife in the air. "Exactly."

I put another handful of beans in a jar. "I don't know about that, Ruth. For one thing, Nate confirmed he'd suspected her of killing Darla, so that would have turned Barr's attention to her eventually. And she never got rid of the shovel. They found it in her garden shed. Darla's wallet, too."

Ruth frowned and returned to her cutting board. "Bette always seemed smarter than that."

"I don't think it was about being smart or dumb," I said. "It was about feeling bad. She wanted to confess." And she wanted to pay for what she'd done. Hadn't even tried to make bail.

When I'd gone to Bette's to pick up Alexander and bring him home, I'd found the mask of Barr's face. Even though she'd said she couldn't sculpt it from a photo, Bette had created a very realistic representation of his face from the picture his mother had taken at our wedding ceremony. It was pure genius, truly a gorgeous piece.

I'd wrapped it in several layers of paper and put it in the back of the closet in our sitting room. No one knew it was there except me, and I had no idea what to do with it. It would be too weird to give it to Barr for his birthday now, and I definitely didn't want a constant reminder of Bette and her sad madness hanging on my wall.

But I couldn't get rid of it, either. At least not yet.

Meghan had grown quiet. "I feel almost sorry for her," she said now.

"I know—" I began.

Barr cut in. "Don't. Bette Anders had some bad things happen to her. Everyone does. That's life. It's no excuse for killing someone."

"You're right, of course," Ruth said. "But not everyone sees the world in such black and white terms."

"That's not—"

"Are you going to get one of those lighters with a camera in it?" I interrupted, leaving my post to look over Kelly's shoulder. Enough talk about death.

"Nah," he said. "Private investigators don't really need most of this stuff, at least not doing the kind of work I do. But since giving up my apartment, I've rented a small office space to work out of, and I need office equipment." He smiled. "And maybe a new digital video camera."

"You don't already use one?" I asked.

"Of course. But sometimes you need a couple of them at the same time." He sat back, tapping his fingers on the table. "You know, there's plenty of work for me in this area, especially now that I got that insurance company contract. There will be times when I'll have to bring someone in to help. Think you might be interested in moonlighting, Sophie Mae?"

"Kelly!" Meghan said.

"You can help, too," he teased.

Barr said. "Are you trying to get my wife into even more trouble than she usually manages?" But he was smiling. Sort of.

I pushed him playfully on the shoulder, and he slid his arm around my waist.

"Well, if I'm going to help you—and I'm not saying I will—then I want the lighter with the camera in it," I said. "It would make me feel like James Bond."

"You'd have to learn how to smoke," Barr teased.

"Hrm. Never mind, then." I pushed away from him and went back to the stove.

Was Kelly serious? I thought he might be. Sophie Mae Ambrose: Private Eye. On assignment, snooping into the lives of strangers—instead of investigating people she knew.

I liked it.

Erin's phone clucked like a chicken.

"That's your ring tone?" I asked.

"My text tone." She looked at Meghan. "Please, Mom? Zoe was going to let me know when she got home from riding."

My friend gave a rueful grin. "Go ahead."

I looked around at everyone. My family, I thought. A made family, but close and happy. With the addition of Kelly and Alexander, the house was filled to bursting. There was still room for a baby if that was in the cards, but Barr and I were no longer trying to force the issue.

We hadn't given up, though. After all, if you don't succeed, try, try again.

THE END

RUTH'S PICKLED DILLY BEANS

Makes 7 pint jars.

- 4 pounds perfect, whole green, or wax beans
- 7 small dried or fresh cayenne peppers OR 1¾ teaspoons hot pepper flakes
- 7 whole cloves of peeled garlic
- 7 fresh dill heads OR 3½ teaspoons dried dill seeds
- 5 cups water
- 5 cups vinegar
- 7 Tablespoons pickling salt
- 7 wide-mouth pint jars with lids and sealers

Wash beans thoroughly. Snap ends and cut to uniform lengths to fit upright in the pint jars, allowing one inch of headroom.

Sterilize jars and lids, leaving lids and sealers in scalding water until ready to use.

Into each jar place a pepper (or ¼ teaspoon hot pepper flakes), a clove of garlic, and a head of dill (or ½ teaspoon of dill seed). Pack the beans into the jars, leaving an inch of headroom.

Heat the water, vinegar, and salt together. After it reaches a boil and the salt is dissolved, pour it over the beans. Be sure to leave ½ inch of headroom. Run a knife or sterilized skewer around the edge to remove air bubbles and secure the lids.

Process in a 185° F water bath for 10 minutes after the water in the canner returns to a simmer. Add one minute of processing time for every 1,000 feet in altitude. Remove the jars and complete the seals if necessary.

Wait a couple of weeks before trying these out. The flavors will intensify with time. These are a perfect addition to a Bloody Mary!

SOPHIE MAE'S CSA KALE CHIPS

1 bunch of any kind of kale (6–8 ounces)
1 Tablespoon of olive oil
Salt to taste

Preheat the oven to 350° F. Wash the kale and dry *thoroughly*. Using a salad spinner is ideal. Remove the stems and tough ribs from the kale and tear into three-to-four-inch pieces. Toss with the olive oil. Continue until the kale is lightly coated all over. Add salt to taste and toss some more to evenly distribute.

Lay the seasoned kale out in a single layer on a cookie sheet covered with non-stick aluminum foil or parchment paper. Bake for 8–10 minutes in preheated oven. Start checking at 8 minutes—some chips will crisp faster than others. You don't want to burn them.

You can use more than one cookie sheet or work in batches. Allow to cool, then store in an airtight container for a week or more (if they last that long). Kale chips can also be frozen in zippered plastic bags or lidded containers.

For more variations, try hazelnut or walnut oil instead of olive oil, and use smoked or otherwise flavored salt—or even a little lemon zest—to add some extra zing. There are lots of different kinds of kale, and all make good chips. However, cooking times may differ a little between varieties.

Photograph by Kevin Brookfield

ABOUT THE AUTHOR

Cricket McRae's interest in traditional colonial skills is reflected in her contemporary Home Crafting Mysteries. Set in the Pacific Northwest, they feature everything from soap making to food preservation, spinning to cheese making. For more information about Cricket, go to her website, www.cricketmcrae.com, or her blog, www.hearthcricket.com.